OBSESSED

Also by March Hastings

Abnormal Wife
Again and Again
The Boys of Brigham Dee
By Flesh Alone
Crack-Up
The Demands of the Flesh
Design for Debauchery
Enraptured
Fear of Incest
The Heat of the Day
Her Private Hell
The Jealous and Free
Obsessed
The Outcasts
A Rage Within
Savage Surrender
The Soft Way
Three Women
The Third Sex
The Third Theme
The Unashamed
Veil of Torment
Whip of Desire

OBSESSED

MARCH HASTINGS

CUTTING EDGE

ISBN-13: 978-1-952138-87-4

Published by
Cutting Edge Books
PO Box 8212
Calabasas, CA 91372
www.cuttingedgebooks.com

CHAPTER ONE

SHE looked up at the nameplate. The name Milton V. Ross, M.D. glinted reassuringly in the pale October sunlight. Sue Ellen spelled out the letters to herself. A nervous warmth made her skin moist beneath the cashmere sweater. But along with this nervousness, she felt a deep calm. It was the deadly calm of desperation. For Sue Ellen knew that if Dr. Ross couldn't help her, she would very quietly take an overdose of sleeping pills and rid herself forever of the endless, gnawing desire.

But she didn't want to die. And so she stepped quickly inside the building and climbed the flight of pleasant grey carpeting to keep her appointment.

A buxom nurse sat behind a small wooden desk, her starched uniform stretched almost beyond capacity. She looked up at Sue Ellen and smiled warmly, as a great aunt might smile at a favorite niece.

"Good afternoon. I'm Sue Ellen Gaynor." She hesitated, knowing of course that this woman could not know the reason for her visit. And yet, since there were literally hundreds of men and women who knew, perhaps this lady had heard it somewhere.

"Miss Gaynor, the doctor will be with you in a moment. Won't you be seated?"

"Thank you."

Sue Ellen felt better. The nurse had spoken to her as though she were a normal human being. To eat, to sleep a full night restfully. She found a red leather chair and crossed her legs automatically as she sat down. This movement of her legs was a little trick she had acquired somewhere in the befuddled past. Her thighs pressed tightly together. Her nerves shivered in response. Someday, if God were with her, it would stop pulsing there. Someday, she would stop riding subways just for the sensation of rubbing herself against a stranger.

She picked up a copy of *Time* from the low table beside her. The magazine opened almost by itself because she wasn't concentrating on it. The quiet room with its soft leathers and polished woods was a good place to read. But her troubled mind raced backward into time, searching for important facts to tell the doctor. Where was the beginning? When was the seed of the serpent planted within her? Perhaps she should start with her earliest memory...

"Miss Gaynor?"

Sue Ellen glanced upward from her thoughts to Dr. Ross standing in the doorway. The light filtering in from behind him made his stocky person seem to lean toward her. His grey hair cut very short gave him a wise but youthful appearance.

She put aside the magazine and stood up. Clutching her purse, Sue Ellen realized that her palms were soaking wet. She wanted to turn and run. Where would she find the courage to speak of the phantasies and the truths of her existence? Her heart beat wildly in her chest. The satin brassiere became tight and seemed to cut into her ribs. But oddly, her legs were carrying her toward Dr. Ross.

Inside there were no mirrors for her to see if her long hair was still neatly combed or if she had bitten off the inside of her orange lipstick.

Dr. Ross closed the door. And now she was alone with the soft blue walls, the diplomas hanging in frames, the view between grey curtains of clouds and sky. The doctor...and herself.

Instinctively she went for the leather couch and lay down on it as the doctor seated himself behind his desk.

Yet in a second she was sitting up again, her hands folding and unfolding as though searching for something to hold onto that would not escape her.

"Maybe I'm making a mistake," she blurted. "Maybe you can't help me at all." She waited for him to deny this, to reassure her.

"Miss Gaynor, before we come to any decisions, let me tell you something about the methods and goals of psychoanalysis." He took a package of Camels from his desk drawer and pulled off the red band of cellophane. "It is a lengthy and expensive and arduous process. You will have to learn how to be completely honest during our talks. The better you can learn to report every passing mood, every thought and thought fragment, the sooner we can discover your patterns and reconstruct them."

Sue Ellen listened carefully. She knew that Dr. Ross was not a beginner and that he had a wide reputation in his profession. But he was, after all, a man. And men had that certain something that she had never been able to forget, even for an instant. Perhaps it would have been better to consult with a woman. Yet women were no better. She couldn't trust anybody. Least of all herself. She must believe in Dr. Ross. Or…

"I'll do anything you say," she admitted softly.

"Right at first, I ask only that you try not to hold anything back."

"Well, I'm going half out of my mind," she said shakily. "I'm a nymphomaniac. That's what they call me."

"What do you mean when you say nymphomaniac?" He leaned forward and extended the cigarettes to her.

She noticed the buffed fingernails, so clean, so pink and white. "You have nice hands," she said. "I like clean hands."

He nodded in approval. "That's the idea. Anything that comes into your mind."

Sue Ellen remembered the question. "I mean I'm always…sexed up. Throbbing…" Her voice shook. "…there. It's like a mouth always open, wanting to be fed. Never satisfied.

Never enough food." She let herself relax back onto the couch. This way she could not see the doctor's face. She was remembering ...

"Sue Ellen! Chil', where you got yourself at? Come inside this instant, hear?"

Sue Ellen heard very well. But she didn't want to go inside. She snuggled up closer on the lap of her Daddy and listened to the gentle creaking of the swing as his long legs rocked them. She watched the shadow of the maple trees roll back and forth over her dress. The smell that came from her father's scraggle of red beard was nicer than all the com pudding that Clellie could bake.

"Better go now, honey."

"No." Sue Ellen shut her eyes tight and flung her arms around her father's neck. "I won't go. I don't want to. Please say I don't have to go. Daddy, please." Her voice was high pitched and tense. Her body felt like the whistle that blew from the factory every day at noon.

She did not understand why the valises had been taken out of the closet. For over a week she had watched Mamma emptying drawers, filling trunks with dresses and underwear and stockings. But Daddy hadn't put any of his clothes into the travelling bags. He'd just sat around the house letting his beard grow longer and listening to Mamma giving Clellie orders to get train tickets and make sure about reservations.

Clellie came around now to the front of the house. She stood on the lawn, hands on hips, her ebony face gleaming as if it had just been rubbed with oil.

"No time for lazin'," she said, her deep voice velvety with a sudden tenderness.

"I hate up North!" Sue Ellen cried, her arms tightening their hold. She thought of icebergs and blizzards and angry polar bears.

"You'll like New York, darling. It's a fine, wonderful place with lots of toys and lots of people."

She felt his chest stiffen and the strong muscles of his fingers undoing her grip from around his neck. He lifted her off his lap and set her on the floor. "Go on now. Your mother's waiting."

Sue Ellen glared at him, believing now in her rush of anger all the bad words her mother called him. They were bad words, not because she knew what they meant, but because of Mamma's voice when she used them.

"Undersexed!!" Sue Ellen parroted her mother. "Undersexed dwunken bastid."

She turned and fled toward the warm softness of Clellie's apron.

"Tell me what you're feeling," the doctor said. His voice was non-committal. Neither anxious nor hurrying.

"I was just remembering about when my mother and father separated. That was the last time I had an honest to goodness Southern style dinner. I took a trip down South a few years ago. But it wasn't the same. Maybe I just couldn't appreciate it anymore. Like believing in Santa Claus."

"How old were you when your parents separated?"

"Six. I don't want to talk about that. I want you to stop me from … showing myself to strangers. One of these days, you know what I'm going to do? I feel it coming on. It's like a fever. I'm going to sit on the train and spread my legs so men can look up there. Like my brother used to look up the maid's dress when she climbed a ladder to change a bulb. I'm going to spread my legs and pull my skirt way up over my legs and scream out anybody can have it that wants it." Sue Ellen brought her palm quickly up to her mouth and pressed it hard against her lips.

Yet strangely she felt relieved to have said the words out loud. She lay quietly now for a minute, just feeling the pressure in her mind dwindle. An abstract painting hung on the wall above her feet and her eyes wandered aimlessly over the design. For five minutes more she said nothing, abandoned to the sensation of growing lightness. The doctor remained quiet too. Nothing intruded its presence into Sue Ellen's realization.

"No I won't, either," she said at last. "I don't have to do anything I don't want to do."

With a rush of joy it became clear to Sue Ellen that her case was not hopeless.

"I can tell you now about my train trip to New York with my mother."

Mother had gotten her to put on the crinoline slip that tickled when she walked. Wearing her party dress for the journey was supposed to be a reward and an incentive to behaving like a grown-up. Sue Ellen stood beside Mamma, running her tongue over the grit and soot which was settling on the roof of her mouth. She didn't feel at all like crying or making a fuss about the trip. Her mind avoided recapturing the sight of her father still rocking on the porch, a glass drained to the ice cubes resting on his knee.

Though it was only the middle of the afternoon, Sue Ellen felt very tired as though she herself had carried the valises all the way down to the station. The train was just coming along the tracks now. She watched the great black monster slow panting to a halt. The creaking arm of its wheels braked fast with a quick jerk and squeal. Even Clellie wasn't here to wave good-bye. Mother had insisted against all formal farewells, her powdered features serene in the knowledge that any future would be brighter than the moment being lived.

Mother shaded her eyes with a hand sleek and narrow in pale yellow gloves. Looking up, Sue Ellen could see the smooth underside of her arm. Mamma liked to wear dresses you could almost see through. Everybody always said that Mamma had a pretty figure and could get away with dresses most other ladies wouldn't dare put on.

The gloved hand came down and grasped Sue Ellen's. The smooth material felt almost cool. "Come, dear. We mustn't dawdle."

Sue Ellen let herself be pulled along to the three giant steps leading up into the train car. A conductor reached out and swung her into the car. She caught a flash of numbers on the metal piece of his cap.

"Say thank you to the gentleman," her mother said, smoothing down her skirt after navigating the steps.

Sue Ellen mumbled a thank you. Once more the gloved hand found hers. Though she was being held tightly, Sue Ellen had the feeling her mother didn't really know she was there. She thought that her mother could be holding onto a broom stick and not know the difference. They pushed along the aisle past seated people sipping orangeade from paper cups. A fat man was sleeping with his head fallen against the window sash. He made little snoring sounds like a hippopotamus having bad dreams. The smell of half eaten food and cigarette smoke and dust was like a blanket.

"You can sit by the window and watch the scenery. It'll be an education."

Sue Ellen wiggled herself onto the plush green seat and found that her dress clung fast to it. Her legs dangled uncomfortably, unable to touch the floor.

"Now settle down, dear."

Sue Ellen found a bit of ledging and put one foot on it. She heard her mother's purse unclick, then the compact taken out and that unclicked. It was a familiar series of sounds in the unfamiliar atmosphere of the heat congested train. But the sound brought back others, even more familiar and certainly dearer. Her father's metal fishing box jiggling around in the back seat of the car. The plunk-plunk of their hooks and weights as they cast into the lake. She gazed out beyond the little train station toward the violet hills blending with the bright sky.

"All a-board!"

The train shuddered and slid forward.

Sue Ellen's chest felt tight with a sensation she could neither express nor understand.

Her vision seemed to become blurred by the succession of telephone poles whizzing past and Sue Ellen tired of trying to look at the scenery. Her glance went down to the toes of her own patent leather shoes and across to her mother's tan pumps molded gracefully to her feet, crossed at the ankles. The bright flashes of sun had subsided to a dull orange and pink which washed in now from the opposite windows.

"It's pretty nearly time for supper," her mother said, breaking a silence of hours between them.

"I don't think I'm hungry."

"Nonsense. You're always hungry. And going on a trip is very different from being at home." Her cream colored fingers moved up along the back of her neck, fluffing out the waves of silver blonde hair. Sue Ellen waited for her to take out the compact again, but she didn't. Instead she got up and led Sue Ellen to a tiny room which contained a sink and flush bowl. Sue Ellen waited while her mother framed the seat with pieces of tissue.

But even her bladder refused to cooperate. At last she managed, then washed her hands and they went out to the dining car.

As the waiter left with their order, Sue Ellen's gaze fixed on a man sitting diagonally opposite them. He was alone at a little table and was leaning on one elbow, smiling at Sue Ellen. He had dark red hair.

"That man looks like Daddy."

She heard her mother sigh. "I might as well tell you now, since your mind is on it. Though I wanted it to be a surprise for you." She took a gold cigarette case from her purse. Sue Ellen knew by this action that she was about to hear something very important. Her mother only smoked when she had very big surprises indeed.

"Is Daddy coming up North too?"

"Sue Ellen. Dear. Listen to me carefully." She lit the matching gold lighter and brought the tip of the flame quickly to meet the cigarette. The lids fluttered anxiously over her green eyes. They were dark and intense.

"A gentleman is going to meet us when we reach New York. His name is Martin Hurley. He is a very nice person with a big house and a little boy just a few years older than you. We are going to live with Martin and Jeff because Martin is your new father. You're going to have a new father and a brother all at once. Won't that be wonderful?"

The man across the way was still leaning on his elbow but the smile had left his eyes.

"I know you love your Daddy," her mother added quickly. "But we all grow up and change, you know. And I expect that you'll love your new Daddy after awhile, even more. Certainly it will be a good change for you."

Sue Ellen had listened to every word but they were like balls which hit her ears and bounced off again.

"Two Daddies?" she said. She saw her mother's nostrils quiver.

"Well, you can call him Martin, if you prefer."

"I don't know him," she said simply. "And I don't need two Daddies. I wish..." Her words stopped because the man across the way was shaking his head no, as though cautioning her not to say anything bad.

"It's going to be a lot of fun for you." She patted Sue Ellen's arm. "Of course it's going to be a little strange at first. New people. A new town. But Mother is doing the right thing. You'll see."

The man with the red hair winked and nodded at Sue Ellen. She wanted to wink back but both eyes closed at the same time.

"What's the matter with you?" her mother said.

"Nothing." The man played games just like her father. It was fun.

When the waiter returned with the fried chicken, Sue Ellen decided that she'd better try to eat. She didn't want her mother to scold her in front of her new friend.

9

The food went down in lumps and lay tightly wadded in her stomach. She made the feeling worse with swallows of cold milk. It wasn't long before she had to excuse herself from the table, assuring her mother that she could find the washroom all by herself.

Alone in the cubby hole, she shut her eyes tight and waited. When she came out again, white but feeling better, the man with the red hair was coming along the corridor.

"How are you feeling?" he said, bending down so she could look directly into his brown eyes.

"Better, thank you."

"Maybe you'd like a cherry candy. To take away the taste." He reached into his jacket pocket and brought out a roll of candies.

Sue Ellen took one and peeled it slowly, remembering to say thank you.

"New York is a very nice place for little girls," he said. "You're going to make lots of new friends, I'm sure. Then it will be Christmas and Santa Claus …"

Sue Ellen's fear and tension and bewilderment came to a sudden climax. The man's face blurred and swam in her vision.

When she came awake, she was being carried by strong arms that nestled her like a baby. She didn't care that the sight of her like this would make her mother angry. The one thing she knew was a peaceful sensation of comfort more necessary to her than food or sleep or a thousand new friends. Sue Ellen closed her ears to the thousand questions and pardons her mother effused. Promptly she was taken off to bed, a narrow place behind dark curtains.

A half moon rode among millions of blue white stars. Sue Ellen smiled, not at the moon, but at a new understanding. She had always been cautioned never to take candy from a stranger. But strangers could be nicer than your own mother. Sue Ellen decided that she liked strangers. And she knew that New York would be full of them.

CHAPTER TWO

D r. Ross had arranged three appointments a week with her. Sue Ellen came to the second one anxious to go on with her story. The past held many discomforts. But as she was slowly beginning to relive those years, they presented many pleasures also, pleasures which in her anxiety she had neglected to consider.

"Did you ever see the red haired man again?" Dr. Ross asked, wiping his glasses and placing them carefully on the blotter of his desk.

"No. I didn't even see him get off the train."

So many things appeared to be happening at Pennsylvania Station that if she wasn't careful the crowd would sweep her away. All the people in the world seemed to have been dropped right here in the middle of the station and commenced to make as much noise as they possibly could. And everybody seemed in such a terrible hurry to go upstairs or downstairs or onto an escalator or into a waiting train. It was a wonder that Martin Hurley found them within ten minutes after they posted themselves near the information counter.

He was a tremendous sized man and looked like a whale swimming through the crowd. The light blue suit and starched shirt carried about them an odor of flowers, Sue Ellen thought, as she put out her hand to shake with him and received a kiss on the cheek instead. His chin didn't scratch the way her father's did. Martin's skin was very smooth and tight across his cheekbones and nose and chin. He had a happy and smiling look like the face on a Coca Cola ad.

"Come on. We'll catch a taxi and get out of this heat," he said. His voice sounded like it was rattling in a big empty barrel.

"It's all right," she heard her mother say. "I told Sue Ellen all about her new brother and her new father."

"I guess it is," Martin answered.

Sue Ellen watched him put his arms around her mother's waist and press his lips against hers. She wondered why her mother suddenly didn't care about getting her dress creased.

"Well then," her mother said, when they finally drew apart. "You certainly are going to make a good father."

Sue Ellen didn't see what was so funny as she watched both the grown-ups laugh.

Martin attended to the luggage and steered everyone to a waiting cab. Mobs of automobiles appeared to be riding almost on top of each other in a veil of thick smog that only Sue Ellen seemed to notice. Inside the cab, Martin put his arm around Sue Ellen and began telling her all about Jeff.

"Is he as big as you?" she asked. Martin had very blue eyes with a rim of black that seemed to put the final touch of neatness to his appearance. He stretched out his legs and touched the driver's seat with the soles of his white shoes. She hoped he would be very careful so nobody would step on them and make a smudge.

"Oh, not quite as big," Martin laughed. "But almost."

She hoped Jeff would be big enough, at least, to carry her if she decided to faint again. It was a new word and she liked it.

"You'll see for yourself very soon," her mother said. "It's going to be wonderful, just like I told you." She ran her hand up along the back of her neck in the nervous motion Sue Ellen understood without knowing, then let her fingers fall, as if by accident, to rest on the side of Martin's thigh. "Everything is going to be wonderful ... again." Her voice had a queer husky sound.

Sue Ellen was busy watching people dash between cars and come out safe on the other side of the street. For a moment she was vibrantly awake, as though a heavy door had closed on all the yesterdays. The ticklish crinoline had flattened out from all the sitting, she had a happy man beside her who promised to be fun. Maybe, if she tried very hard, she could write a letter telling Daddy about all the wonderful things that were happening and he would come to New York too. She promised herself not to forget one single moment of her adventures so she would be able to make the letter very exciting.

The cab pulled up in front of a large canopied house that rose endlessly into the sky. Across the street ran a grey wall of stone which fenced off trees proud of their thick green foliage.

"That's Central Park," Martin said. "Jeff will take you to the Zoo and to the merry-go-round."

They rode up many floors in an elevator that carried them slickly aloft. Then Martin was ringing the bell of a polished black door trimmed with gold.

A boy with sunburned skin opened the door. Every inch of him was the color caramel except for the brief white tennis shorts. He wore nothing else.

"Hi," he said. "You're Margaret, aren't you?" He was exactly the same height as Sue Ellen's mother. He had streaks of hair bleached just as silver from the sun. "Do I get to kiss my new mother?" He reached over and kissed her quickly on the lips before anyone could say a word.

"And this is your new sister," Martin said.

"Hi, Sis. You're pretty too."

Sue Ellen extended her face for him to kiss her also.

"Fast learner," Martin chuckled.

Jeff rumpled her hair instead. "Remind me to take you up on that in a few years."

Sue Ellen's mother lay her purse down on an end table. "What a lovely family we're going to make."

The apartment had nine large rooms and for the first time Sue Ellen had a real bed room without the sound of Clellie's snoring. A bath connected her room with Jeff's on the right side. Her mother and Martin were on the left with a glass-knobbed door separating her room from theirs.

After a day of unsuccessfully trying to be friends with Jeff, Sue Ellen knew that she was very very tired. Her back ached, her legs ached, her throat was slightly sore. But she could not fall asleep. The huge mattress was the softest thing she had ever put her body on, except for the hay mow back home. She spread her arms and her legs wide, stretching the muscles. The sheets were cool and tight and fresh to her skin. The electric fan in the window purred gently. She turned over and stretched again. Her delicate nipples grazed against the edge of the pillow and she shivered in innocence. Yet the room seemed like a huge black lake and she was swimming in the middle of it. The hazy night made dark shadows of the furniture. The mirror reflected lights from a distant part of the city like a thousand wild eyes. Sue Ellen sat up.

She swung her legs over the side of the bed and went to the window, thinking about what she was going to say in her letter to Daddy. Absolutely, she mustn't tell him that Jess thought she was still a baby. No. She would tell him how she could see the lake in Central Park from her window and that she was going fishing there every day. With her forearms resting on the windowsill, she tried to believe that it wasn't really lonely here at all. She remembered dimly her mother's weekend trip, the words Mexican divorce and remarriage which she had heard between Mother and Daddy. They had meant nothing to her at the time.

Her silent thoughts were interrupted by a voice coming from behind the door with the glass knob. Unconsciously her ears alerted for human companionship in the vast darkness. A bed began to thump on well softened springs.

"Oh, darling ... take me." It sounded like her mother's voice except it was too harsh and raspy. Maybe they had turned on a radio. She edged closer to the door, listening.

More thumps of the bedspring, like when she used to jump on the one back home.

"I want to tease you till you bite." Was this Martin's voice?

"Oh, please. Please."

"Bite me."

"I'll chew you to pieces ... Oh ... oh ... oh, yes."

Sue Ellen sat down on the carpet beside the door, hugging her knees. She wished she could go in and listen. It sounded like a scary program. But fun.

When morning came, Sue Ellen had finally fallen asleep on the edge of her bed. She lay tangled in a sheet and twisted in dreams of racing automobiles that could not stop. She didn't awaken until almost noontime and only then because her mother was trying to move her into the center of the bed. She opened her eyes and found her mother beaming a huge smile.

"My little lazy darling." She leaned over and planted a kiss on Sue Ellen's ear. The ends of her hair were still damp from a freshly taken bath and a bit of powder came off on Sue Ellen's cheek.

"Did my darling have a good night's sleep?"

It wasn't often that she deserved to be called darling and Sue Ellen wondered what she had done to put her mother in such a good mood already. She decided not to tell her about walking around the room in the dark.

"I had a funny dream," she said.

"Well, we all have funny dreams now and then. Now come along and we'll give you a nice bath. Jeff said he would take you to the beach today."

"Jeff doesn't like me very much."

"What makes you say such a silly thing? Of course he does."

She wanted desperately for Jeff to like her. He wasn't as big as Martin, but he certainly was big enough for Sue Ellen until she grew up. Maybe if she showed Jeff how far she could swim, he would like her better. Instantly she bounded out of bed and waited while her mother ran water into the bathtub.

Afterward she drank orange juice and downed a soft boiled egg at the long table in the dining room. While she ate, Jeff made a phone call. She listened to him telling a friend that he was bringing along his new kid sister. His voice sounded pleased about the idea. They grinned at each other.

Martin had gone to the office, but he had sent back the limousine to take the children to the beach. Wearing a green playsuit buttoned over her bathing togs, Sue Ellen got into the back seat with Jeff, telling him in a long stream of chatter about how she had swum back and forth across the lake at home, which was surely as big as the ocean.

He listened good-naturedly and didn't seem to doubt one word of her story. Encouraged Sue Ellen made the lake a little larger and told him about another time when she had saved a little girl who had fallen out of a boat.

Jeff said, "I'm a Junior Life Saver." He pushed down his tennis shorts and showed her the emblem sewn onto his suit.

Sue Ellen examined it gravely. Her inclination to describe further exploits dwindled.

"I got that at camp last year," Jeff continued. "That's when I was only ten. Maybe next summer you can go to camp too. Anyway, you're going to like my father a heck of a lot. Men are nicer than women. I'd rather have a father than a mother any time. Women are weak. They're always getting sick or dying or something."

Sue Ellen agreed with him about men. Vaguely, she wished that it were possible for her to grow up to be a father. She knew there was some kind of difference between boys and girls that had nothing to do with hair styles. And this difference would make her grow up to be a mother instead. Maybe if she knew more, she could do something about it.

These thoughts ran swiftly through her head, too complicated to find expression. They came to rest beyond the area of her imagination, waiting as though behind a dark wall to leap again and find satisfaction.

The limousine made its way out of the city traffic and pulled up finally in front of a large bath house constructed on a wide expanse of private beach. Jeff opened the door and leaped out, yelling, "C'mon."

Sue Ellen raced after him trustingly. He took her to an attendant, who in turn led her into a locker room and slipped an elastic band with a key attached around her ankle. The damp room was filled with maybe half a dozen women in various conditions of undress. One lady was standing in front of a mirror attached to her locker door, massaging cream into the generous soft flesh of her breasts.

"What's that for?" Sue Ellen inquired.

"Oh, it keeps you from getting irritations, honey."

Sue Ellen hadn't meant the cream. But she decided not to ask any more questions and proceeded to struggle with the buttons of her play suit. Mother seldom showed her nakedness to Sue Ellen and the idea of carrying around those huge lumps of jiggly flesh fascinated her. She hadn't decided whether they were good things to possess or not. Her own flat chest with its pink buds of nipples seemed much more agreeable. Certainly more like a man's and therefore better. Anyway she never got irritations.

She stuffed her playsuit and sneakers and socks into the locker, slapped the door shut and went back outside to find Jeff. The attendant gave her a towel on the way out and she draped it around her neck, the way her Daddy did when they went swimming together.

Jeff was waiting for her beside the concrete steps leading down to the sand. He stood talking to a group of three other boys, all of them dressed in navy blue suits which emphasized the thinness of their young chests and that little bit of a bulge between their legs which made them able to go to the bathroom standing up. She thought it very unfair of her mother not to have given her one of those things also.

"There she is," she heard Jeff say. "Isn't she a cutey?"

Sue Ellen felt like a puppy must feel in the first wonderful days of being a novelty. She skipped over to Jeff, who said, "This is Richard, this is Paul, this is Chipper."

She smiled around dizzily at all three, hardly believing that she could be the center of such wonderful company. Jeff and Richard each took one of her hands and swung her down the steps. She giggled wildly. They ran down to the edge of the surf, flung their towels backward at the sand and splashed into the small rolling crests. The glittering water shocked her with its iciness. The soles of her rubber swim shoes grazed along rolling shells. Her hands, beating at the surge of foam, splashed salty drops into her own open mouth and eyes. Breathless she laughed and shrieked.

It seemed hardly a moment later when the sound of a police whistle caught her attention. Paul and Chipper were off at a distance, trying to stand on their hands in the waves. Again the whistle blew.

"Have that kid dry out for awhile!" The command came from a man in an orange bathing suit sitting high high up on a white chair.

Jeff grabbed Sue Ellen around the waist and brought her out on the sand. Richard came with him, flinging his sogged black curls back from his forehead.

"You stay with her," Jeff said. "I'll go get an umbrella." The smile was gone from his face, his lips thin with annoyance. He jogged back to the bathhouse, dripping dark splotches into the sand behind him.

Richard put a towel over Sue Ellen's head and began to rub it. "I'm okay," she insisted, shivering.

"Yeah, your lips are blue." He had very brown eyes that rested with velvet patience on Sue Ellen.

She didn't try to argue with him, but abandoned herself to the feel of the Turkish towel rubbing and patting against her skin. The sun soon warmed her shoulders and except for the cold dampness of her suit and the drops of water running down the inside of her thighs, she was soon comfortable.

Jeff returned carrying a green and white striped umbrella. He worked its wooden stem into the sand and sat her in its scalloped shade. "I got some Noxema too," he said.

Richard took the blue jar, unscrewed the cap and rubbed cream on Sue Ellen's back.

"Now you stay here," Jeff said.

Helplessly, she watched him go off with Richard. His voice drifted back to her ... "Girls are a pain."

Pain ... Sue Ellen's mind stopped remembering. The sound of a bus turning clumsily around a corner intruded itself into the office. She let her arm fall down and dangle off the edge of the couch.

"Dr. Ross, I feel like giggling," she said.

"Well giggle then."

"I can't. But I want to." She heard him unscrew the cap of his fountain pen.

"What are you thinking? What's funny?"

"Jeff ... Richard ... girls are a pain. That's funny. I guess I must have been a pain for a few years, though. Until I started developing hips. Lumps. I mean breasts. I think of them as lumps. Sometimes, when I'm alone, I touch them myself so the nipples will stand up. It's very comforting. My mother was a flat-chested type. I don't think she liked the idea that I was going to outdo her that way."

Sue Ellen had just passed her eleventh birthday when her mother decided that it was about time she start wearing a bras-siere. Five years of living in the luxurious comforts provided by

Martin's generosity had taught Sue Ellen a very strong lesson. To have a man was to have the world. She liked to sit on Martin's lap and distract his attention from everything and everybody else. When he would come home in the evening, she was the first one to run and kiss him.

Her mother laughed and said it was cute. At first. But along with the brassiere came a lecture in deportment. She was now forbidden to throw herself at Martin.

But Sue Ellen had learned another lesson too. And that was that her mother did not have the last word. Martin was the boss. His word was law. She decided that she was going to find out from Martin himself whether or not she had to stop sitting on his lap.

With the shrewdness of her burgeoning womanhood, Sue Ellen first went and combed her hair with special neatness. She pinned the blonde tresses back with some of her mother's bobbies. Then she dabbed cologne around the stray whisps of her neckline. The new brassiere confined her too tightly. She found it difficult to breathe. The satin material was really quite soft but it irritated her nipples strangely. She felt ill at ease in the area of her young breasts. The bathroom light reflected her cheeks rouged with the cosmetics of sun and air and girlhood. Her shiny nose was beginning to take shape out of its button blob. She licked her lips to make them shiny, not daring to apply any of her mother's make-up. But she wasn't satisfied with the result. Carefully she put a little bit of lipstick on the end of her pinky and rubbed it into her lips, gaining just enough color so that no one could tell if they didn't look too hard.

Then she went into the living room and paraded around, swinging the fullness of her skirts in movie star fashion. Her mother was at Saks Fifth Avenue shopping for a birthday present for Richard's mother. Alone in the house, Sue Ellen played the game of being an adult.

The unexpected appearance of Jeff startled her in her play acting. She stood in the center of the carpet, a little embarrassed, a little annoyed.

"What's all this?" Jeff said, flinging down his books and staring with a broad smirk at the newly molded points in Sue Ellen's blouse.

"I thought you were at football practice," she said in a low voice over which she didn't have much control.

"Strained my ankle. Coach told me to stay shy of it for a week. Say, don't turn your back on me. I didn't get a good look yet."

He hobbled over to her and touched her shoulder with a tentative finger. "You smell different. Funny."

"I do not." Her voice was suddenly too loud. She whirled around to face him. Behind the smile in his eyes, she saw the tautness of pain. He limped a few steps backward from her.

At sixteen Jeff was well on his way to manhood. He shaved the mustache on his upper lip so that it wouldn't make an ugly smudge. Sports had built a thick sturdiness into his chest. And he was almost six feet tall already.

"Does your foot hurt a lot?"

"It's nothing."

"Sit down and take off your shoe."

Embarrassed now himself, Jeff sat down on the couch. The living room was a place of overstuffed chairs and French lace. The comfortable plushness seemed to muffle their awkward antagonisms.

"Come on," she said, "let me see."

But Jeff wouldn't move to unlace his shoe. He could only sit very still, examining Sue Ellen who was no longer the kid sister that was a general nuisance and pest.

Sensing his resistance, Sue Ellen bent over and unlaced the shoe herself. She lifted the ankle and placed it on her lap, touching it gently. Jeff winced.

"I said it was okay," he protested.

"You're lying."

"Well, all it needs is a hot soak and it'll be good as new. Coach said so himself."

"All right then. Stay here." She went off to the kitchen and filled a basin with hot water and carried it carefully back to the living room.

Ignoring his fragments of protests, she pulled off the sock and rolled up the cuff of his slacks. A peculiar sensation thrilled through her as her fingers touched the hair on his leg. She put his foot slowly into the water and saw his calf tighten against the sting of the heat.

"Thanks," he grumbled. "I didn't mean to be such a sissy."

She was still on her knees beside the basin. She had an odd desire to put her cheek against the curling hairs.

"You're not a sissy," she said, "you're an ape." Her hand slid up along the material of his trousers, propelled by a mysterious urge. "I wish you really liked me and didn't always call me names and things." The autumn sky painted hazes of pastel across his face as she looked up at him.

He didn't answer.

Still in kneeling position, she rested her forearms on Jeff's lap. She felt his thighs pulsing. Her own body pulsed in ryhthm. But a wall of pride stopped her from betraying her feelings any further. She rose quickly to her feet and started to walk away.

"Hey, wait a minute," he called.

Sue Ellen turned.

"Didn't your mother ever tell you anything about boys?"

"Of course she did," Sue Ellen lied. Many times her mother had tried to say something, but her sentences broke off into stammers and finally trailed away in senseless fluttering ribbons of tone. What she knew about boys came from the whispered confidences of schoolmates. The subject had left Sue Ellen curious and anxious for revelation.

"Well … you're not supposed to tease." He folded his arms and tried to look important. The red stripes in his sports sweater matched the color which suffused his cheeks.

"I didn't mean to do that," she said, a tremor of pleasure rippling along her back. "It's just that I'm … growing up." She put her hands on her hips. "And you should begin to treat me like a lady."

"Bro-ther!"

Sue Ellen knew in a flash that she had made progress with Jeff. Encouraged she came back and sat down on the couch beside him.

"Don't you want to smell me again?" Her voice was kittinish. She tilted her neck toward his nose.

Hesitantly he leaned toward her. She saw his hand begin to lift, return toward his lap, then come up and suddenly find a resting place on her waist. An outline of goose pimples popped all around the area of his touch. The hand began to move upward till it reached the lower edge of her bra. Sue Ellen caught her breath. In a sudden jump, his palm was pressing her breast.

"Jesus," he breathed. "You are a big girl."

Her throat was tight. Her breath caught and jerked out in shallow gasps. She had a sudden yearning to touch him back. As though reading her thoughts, he took her hand with his free one. A moment of hesitation made her rigid. Then the lure of her curiosity overcame all fear.

A key rattled in the door. They jumped apart.

They were both very well composed when Sue Ellen's mother came in. But this new revelation about men made Sue Ellen pause to consider the actual wisdom of continuing to sit on Martin's lap.

CHAPTER THREE

"That day with Jeff started me off," Sue Ellen said.

"Don't you think that adolescent sex play is normal?" The scrape of a match accompanied Dr. Ross's question.

"Yes. Up to a point, though. You see, Jeff was no slacker. And I was a very good partner, a willing partner to all the games he devised. That very night he took me to a movie. But not to see the picture."

Both Mother and Martin thought it was wonderful that Jeff was interested enough to start taking Sue Ellen along with him.

They bundled into heavy coats and went to a theater on Lexington Avenue. It wasn't so cold that they needed those long coats, but after they found seats Sue Ellen understood why Jeff had insisted. He folded his on his lap and made her do the same. Only a few moments passed before she felt his hand creeping along between her coat and skirt. She swallowed hard and waited. He didn't try to edge her skirt up so he could get his hand beneath, but contented himself with molding the material so that it squeezed between her legs like a pair of slacks. The sensation of his curious fingers searching out that area of her body tensed her with a series of tremors that made her mouth dry. With assumed casualness, Sue Ellen looked about to see if anyone in the audience were noticing. Not a soul was paying them the slightest attention. Jeff had wisely chosen a Cary Grant comedy and everyone in the dark theater seemed intent on what was happening on the screen.

Reassured Sue Ellen let her own hand travel beneath Jeff's coat. Out of a new found passion, her fingers sought him eagerly. Unconsciously she shifted in her seat so that he might touch her better. She lifted her hips as his hand continued to caress her. She felt her body go rigid as a mounting tenseness overwhelmed her. She began to tremble then as the tightness increased beyond reality. Her new brassiere was soaked in perspiration. The movement of her own hand became more rapid. A series of convulsive shocks consumed her. She relaxed. Her hand stopped moving.

Sneaking a look at Jeff, she saw that his eyes were narrowed. He brought her hand back.

Alone in bed that night Sue Ellen had much to think about. But a wave of sleep commanded her.

It was the first really dreamless, rested sleep that Sue Ellen remembered since the day they had left Virginia. Until that night there was nothing to point out the comparison. Nor did she even think about sleep in this way. Her young mind knew only that she had achieved a magnificent restfulness.

The next morning she was happy and miserable all at the same time. Her body felt chipper and carefree. Her conscience dragged with doubts. She was sufficiently educated to understand that her behavior with Jeff was not something she could tell her mother. She dressed, went to school and tried to concentrate on arithmetic.

That evening she avoided Jeff altogether. After supper she went right to her room and opened a history book. She had even avoided kissing Martin hello, for fear that he would sense a knowingness about her.

But despite these conflicts, Sue Ellen knew that she was only delaying her own fun. She had honestly enjoyed the adventure with Jeff. It couldn't make babies, she knew. So in the back of her mind she waited for Friday evening when Martin habitually took her mother to a supper club.

It helped a little for Sue Ellen to know that Jeff wasn't in the least disturbed by what they had done. And it made him more interested in her generally. If she wanted to talk to him about a geography composition, he was more than willing to work out the assignment with her. The experiment had given Sue Ellen a new status.

When Friday arrived, she and Jeff waited like two crouching tigers for their parents to leave. The minute the door closed they collided, as though by pre-arrangement, in the living room.

But facing each in the light affected their brashness. Sue Ellen delayed by putting on the radio and pretending to search for the Lone Ranger. Jeff went into the kitchen and made them each a glass of chocolate milk. It took a full hour before they were fingering each other again.

Although they had the privacy and freedom of the whole apartment, neither Jeff nor Sue Ellen was particularly anxious to pursue their experiment beyond the touching stage.

"Thinking back to those days," Sue Ellen mused, "I remember them as being the most satisfying in some ways."

"How do you mean?" Dr. Ross was anxious to follow through on this thought. "Tell me what was so especially satisfying."

"I think what I mean is that Jeff's attention and care was what I needed every bit as much as the naive release we got from masturbating each other."

"But you say Martin was attentive to you. And didn't you have friends at school?"

"Yes. I had the usual girl friends. But I always believed that girls were inferior somehow. I don't know why. And Martin was attentive, certainly. But he belonged to my mother. And I sensed even then how possessive she was about him. I assumed she loved him. And that I could understand because of how I loved my father. I think I must have hated my mother very much because she left him."

"Now we're getting somewhere." Dr. Ross's voice sounded pleased. "Perhaps you've noticed how you are inclined to pass over any detailed descriptions of your mother."

"That's true. Mother and I never really paid much attention to each other. Except when we were having arguments. But even then, she wasn't the kind of person to raise her voice. She tried very hard to live up to her image of being a lady."

"What do you mean, lady?"

"I guess mother's conception of a lady was someone who never let feelings get in the way of good manners. She worked hard at achieving serenity. It must have killed her to see me growing up and becoming attractive while her own good looks were fading."

"How did she show this that made it extraordinary?"

"I'm thinking particularly about her relationship with Martin. I've told you how I could hear through that door at night. So what I saw during the day was supplemented by what went on between them when they were in supposed privacy."

Christmas decorations had made their annual fairyland of Fifth Avenue just about the time Sue Ellen had her initiation into sensual pleasure with Jeff. And Martin, for all that he was such a callous businessman in the outside world, had an equally soft heart for Yuletide. During the five years of his marriage, his appearance had taken on a satisfied and prosperous portliness. Sue Ellen's mother was apparently more than adequate in her role as Mrs. Martin Hurley.

But time was beginning to make a few small changes in her too. And they were not changes which added to her serenity. Her blonde hair required attention at the beauty parlor twice a month to keep it looking polished and natural. The face powder which she liked to use profusely was beginning to cake in little pockets around her mouth and in hairfine lines around her eyes. She had a special pumice stone to get the nicotine stains off her fingers.

Sue Ellen noticed these changes only because she could feel a catlike tension almost constantly in her mother's presence. Her mother's irritability made Sue Ellen respond irritably too. And it increased her bad conscience about what was going on between herself and Jeff. Yet underlying everything swept the inevitable tide of maturity overtaking Sue Ellen. She began to think more about clothes and how they draped on her body. She envied adults who could use face powder and mascara and comb their hair up in sleek pompadours. Occasionally she would hear a news commentator reporting on the war in Europe and she would try to conceive of death as something real and able to touch her own life too.

It was a time of growing anxieties and questions for Sue Ellen. The sound of *Come All Ye Faithful* blaring from department stores enticed her to sink into the temporary forgetfulness of buying presents. She asked Martin for permission to use his charge accounts.

They were all seated at the dinner table and Sue Ellen's mother put down her grapefruit spoon with an authoritative clink. "And what makes you think, young lady, that you're old enough to know the value of money?"

It was a question for which Sue Ellen had no answer. "I'll be twelve very soon," she answered quietly, knowing that the reply itself was quite childish.

"Come along, Margaret, this is as good a time as any for Sue to learn." Martin was pouring himself a third glass of sherry and his voice was calm as the blanket of snow lying as white fields in the park.

"I don't know why it gives you such pleasure to spoil her. There's nothing more distasteful than a rich spoiled child."

Jeff tactfully concentrated on the business of heaping sugar on his grapefruit.

"I'm not spoiled and you know it."

"And what do you call answering me in such a tone?"

"Supposing we let the whole thing pass until after dinner," Martin suggested. "This begins to sound like a fishmarket."

Sue Ellen and her mother both subsided dutifully but their exchange of looks promised each other a lively time when they would be alone later on in the evening.

When the table had been cleared, Martin was the first one to bring the subject up again. Seated in his favorite wing chair, he crossed his legs and snipped off the tip of a cigar with his tiny silver folding knife. "Now," he said, surrounding himself in an impenetrable cloud of smoke, "let's try it again. What are your objections, Margaret, to Susie's trying her wings on a shopping spree?"

Sue Ellen's mother was also behind a veil from her own cigarette smoke. Seated at opposite ends of the room, they looked like two little Mounts of Olympus.

"Only that Sue Ellen is still a child. She's not old enough yet to be free from guidance and direction. When I was only eleven, I wouldn't have dared to suggest…"

"That was in the Civil War, my dear," he laughed amiably. "Let's keep up with the times."

Sue Ellen noticed her mother's head begin to tremble. "I'm still young enough indeed," her voice was a trifle shrill. It seemed to make her orange dress vibrate. "You should know that better than anyone."

With a sigh, Jeff sauntered off to his own room.

"I'm sorry you had to take it that way," Martin said. A hint of sadness began to permeate him. "Who knows but that tomorrow none of us will be able to go shopping. President Roosevelt…"

"Politics has nothing to do with this. You're changing the subject."

Sue Ellen hesitated to interfere. But she would have liked to go over to Martin and say something that would comfort him. Instead, she sat very still in one corner of the couch, smoothing the pleats of her grey wool skirt.

"Well, I say that the girl should go out and have some inno-cent fun." It was a statement which allowed for no objection.

Relieved Sue Ellen ran to him instinctively and threw herself at his chest in an impulsive hug of gratitude. "I love you," she whispered in his ear. But it was a whisper that carried around the room.

"Thank heaven you love somebody." Her mother's tone was sour, the words jagged.

Sue Ellen felt loathe to leave the comforting warmth of Martin's presence. She sat down on the bit of chair beside his legs. One of his large hands rested on her shoulder. It had deci-sion and strength and security.

"I'm not going to spend a whole lot of money," she said to him.

"Of course you aren't." He winked and she saw that his eye-lids were a trifle too red.

She tilted her head and rubbed her cheek across the mounds of his knuckles.

He leaned forward and whispered very softly into her ear, "Maybe you'd better buy your mother something extra special."

Sue Ellen nodded.

"Fine manners for people to have secrets," her mother said.

The hours dragged along until bedtime. Sue Ellen undressed quickly, hoping that she could pretend to be asleep when her mother came in to speak with her. But she was just pulling on the bottoms of her pajamas when the door opened.

For a few moments her mother paraded about the room, her hands clasped against her diaphragm, the ash on her cigarette growing longer, unnoticed. Finally she sat down on the edge of the pink stool of Sue Ellen's dressing table.

"My own daughter becoming a stranger to me. You're only eleven years old and I don't know what goes on in your mind anymore. You never speak to me, confide in me. You just might as well not have any mother at all, the way you're behaving."

The upper part of her body was beginning to lean forward, like a sun dial, Sue Ellen thought idiotically.

"I talk to you, mother." She wiggled her feet into sheepskin slippers and went to get the hairbrush from behind her mother's back.

As her hand reached out, her mother's grabbed her wrist and pulled Sue Ellen close. "Now you listen to me. I won't raise any daughter of mine to be a hussy and a man finagler. You're starting at an early age, heaven help me. I can see the signs. And don't try to tell me different. I know my own flesh and blood all right. Sneaking around behind my back, slopping yourself up with perfume not fit for an unmarried woman, let alone a mere infant. You've got your father's taint, but I'll tie you fast to the bedpost before I let you run around contaminating my good name. You don't know what you're doing, poor thing, but listen to me and listen carefully. If I see you playing up to Martin like that once more, you're going away to a boarding school where you'll never see a man until you're old enough to be safely married."

Sue Ellen didn't understand half her mother's words, but she went sick with the fear that somehow she had been spying on her and Jeff. Tears choked up and spilled over. "Don't talk about Daddy," she blurted, hardly realizing that she was thinking about him.

"Just remember, you're a lady if I have to whip you into being one." She let go of Sue Ellen's wrist, leaving red splotches on her flesh. Then she fled from the room, propelled by her own distaste and loathing.

Sue Ellen flung herself on the bed and buried her face in the pillow. The soft goose feathers in their strong ticking muffled her sobs and absorbed the hot flow of misery. Her head throbbed with a violent stabbing which sent shafts of pain along the line of her ribs. She gripped the pillow and pulled it tight to her face, wanting to smother herself.

Gradually the tears subsided. She heard lights being turned off throughout the house. She pulled the quilt up around her shoulders and tried to go to sleep. The greatest hurt of all was that Daddy hadn't answered any of the letters she had written to him throughout the years. Except for Christmas and birthday cards, she never heard from him at all.

At the first sound of footsteps in her mother's bedroom, Sue Ellen pulled the pillow against her ears so she wouldn't hear any more arguing. But she couldn't hold it like that forever.

Their voices were muffled but she heard them distinctly because of her heightened state of tension.

"…Let's not discuss it," her mother was saying. "I think we should save our bedroom for one thing. Help me with these hooks, dear?"

A long silence.

"You're not too tired, darling," her mother's voice again, coaxing. "I know how to wake you up, don't I? Don't I always know what to do to make you feel good?"

"I'm really beat, Margaret. Two weeks in a row…"

"That's what keeps a man virile. Let me just touch you a little."

Sue Ellen dragged the quilt quickly over her head. She wanted to scream.

CHAPTER FOUR

"I believe that was the very first time I thought about sex in connection with my mother."

Dr. Ross dropped a match into the flat porcelain ash tray. It landed with a little clink that sounded very large in the stillness of the office. Sue Ellen noticed for the first time that the ceiling was rather high. This gave her the sensation that she could breath more easily, as though her rib cage was capable of expanding to that distance.

"And I didn't sleep well that night," she added. "In fact I didn't sleep at all."

"What did you do?"

"I kept the quilt wrapped around me very tight. Yes. I rolled myself up inside it like ... like an infant."

"Do you recall what you thought about?" The doctor's voice was casual, but it did not permit her to evade the question.

"I tried very hard not to think. But my mind kept imagining what Mother and Martin were doing in there." Sue Ellen felt a wave of warmth shoot down her back. "I knew it wasn't right. What they did in private was their own business. But I just kept seeing Mother. Naked. Her cool hands along Martin's ..." She could not say the word. "Maybe I was jealous."

"Of whom, your mother or Martin?"

"It's all so jumbled, doctor. As I look back on it, I know that I wanted Martin's affection very much. He could never take the place of my father."

"Did you want him to fondle you? Caress you?"

"Yes. I hate admitting it. That's not a very nice thought, is it? A girl shouldn't want to be in competition with her mother for the same man. And I wasn't even twelve years old!"

"The sexual impulse starts much younger than that." Dr. Ross moved around in his chair and she could hear the leather squeak.

"Sexual impulse. Sex. Sex. Sex. Why is it so fascinating? Hypnotic? It charms like a snake charms a rabbit. I hated myself for thinking about sex. But I didn't really try to stop myself, either. I kept thinking that night what a big man Martin was. How big he must be all over. And the more I thought about it, the more I hated my mother. I thought she was disgusting for doing the very same things that I wanted to do. I couldn't wait until the next time I would be alone with Jeff."

Sue Ellen tried as hard as she could to avoid looking her mother straight in the face the following morning. After eating a hasty breakfast, she rushed off to school.

It was a private school but the rooms were as colorless, the furniture as unimaginative as any public school in the poorest sections of her home town. The teacher's voice was a sprightly drone. It made no more impression on her than the ticking of the dainty watch on her wrist. As Sue Ellen looked at Miss Hawthorne, she began to wonder odd things about her. Like why she wasn't married. If she had a boy friend. If she had ever had a boy friend. Sue Ellen's gaze focused on the little mound of belly which protruded from beneath the belt of the knit suit. But then she deliberately thrust these thoughts aside, ashamed of them, ashamed of herself for thinking this way about a teacher.

She looked around at her classmates, knowing that not a one of them had ever explored the territories she had explored with Jeff. Their shiny heads, neat and bright in the shafts of sunshine slanting in above the window shades, could not be guilty of such thoughts as her own. But nice or not, it was true. She didn't give a hang about geography or grammar. Certain areas of her own body had suddenly grown into adulthood. They demanded to be recognized. And placated.

When three o'clock arrived, she didn't want to face the ordeal of going home. She knew that Jeff had a club meeting at four. Maybe if she phoned him, he would take her along, just this once.

The ice cream parlor was crowded with girls and boys bending straws and telling each other anecdotes about classmates who had ceased being friends. Some of the kids squeezed into a booth motioned to Sue Ellen. She waved back but stayed at a distance, feeling that she really had no place with and no interest in these people. Friends were to confide in, yet she didn't dare reveal any of her secret thoughts. She bought a vanilla cone and waited near the telephone booth until she knew that Jeff would be home from school.

Luckily Jeff answered the ring. Immediately Sue Ellen blurted out the tensions pressing against her conscience about the night before. If anyone could understand, it was Jeff. She could share those thoughts with him because of what they had in common. But though he understood, it wasn't up to him about the club meeting. Girls just weren't allowed in.

"Look," he said, "I'll skip it if you want me to. Suppose I come meet you."

Gratefully Sue Ellen accepted his offer. Besides his voice had a funny tone in it. She had the feeling that he was going to have a long, special talk with her. And she needed someone just now to pay her attention. His concern was making her feel better already. She pulled on her red furry mittens, turned up the collar of her coat and went outside to wait for him.

The December day was crisp and noisy with crowds of out-of-towners. By the time Jeff arrived, Sue Ellen was in a bright mood. She didn't want to talk or think about sex anymore for the afternoon. How nice to link her arm through Jeff's and go crunching over the snow frozen in the park. She wished they had bread crumbs to throw to the lonely sparrows.

They walked past the skating rink and beyond, saying very little to each other in the wake of shouts and squeals from youngsters racing around on the ice. Jeff's hands were pushed deep into the pockets of his leather jacket. She looked up and saw his nose, pink and shiny in the wind. The trees bent and creaked with their burdens of ice. And the air smelled clear as a mountain stream. Though they tramped on with a good deal of space between them. Sue Ellen felt very close to Jeff. Especially since he had given up the club meeting for her. She wanted to rub her cheek against his jacket sleeve.

At last Jeff sat down on the edge of a deserted bench. Sue Ellen took her place beside him, feeling the smooth, iced-over wood against the heavy wool of her coat. She waited happily for anything Jeff wanted to say.

"You're not afraid you're going to be pregnant or anything from that little kidding around we did, are you?" He was sitting with his back to the wind, hunched against it.

"Don't be silly." She tried to laugh nonchalantly.

"What else is there to worry about?"

"I'm not worried, Jeff. I'm …" She couldn't find the word that meant alone and betrayed by her mother, embarrassed by the intimate secrets she had been forced to share through the door.

"Gee whiz, don't tell me you're hot again. Maybe you ought to stop thinking about it. I guess girls are different, though. They don't have to worry about a future. Take me for instance. I have to start studying for college boards pretty soon." His thoughts were centered, not on Sue Ellen, but on himself.

"Girls can have futures too," she objected. "Why, I can be a lawyer or a doctor or anything I want." But privately Sue Ellen had to admit she never gave any thought to a career at all.

"I mean it," he said, his eyes beginning to tear a little from the wind. "I've got to start getting serious. Dad wants me to go to Princeton and my marks aren't half good enough."

"Where's Princeton?"

"New Jersey."

The realization that Jeff would not be living at home any more hit Sue Ellen with full and frightening force. He would be graduating next June. Six months was a very short time. It felt like tomorrow. Jeff going away. Leaving her alone between her mother and Martin. She looked past him to the naked trees standing bleakly against the sky.

"But you'll be coming home for vacations?" she said.

"What are you rushing for?" he said. "I haven't even gotten accepted yet. Let's walk."

She followed him across the park to the West Side exit. Her body felt shivery, chilled clear through to the marrow. Jeff was going to meet other girls. Girls his own age. He would forget all about her.

"You want to go inside someplace where it's warm?" he asked.

She knew what he meant. But they weren't supposed to fool around that way if he had to work on his studies.

"No," she said, "It's no good for you."

"I didn't say that." He took out a pair of white ear muffs and put them on. "I said there's a time and place for that sort of thing."

She wished he would give her some rules for when the time was.

"Come on," he urged. "You know you want to."

Her pride rose stubbornly. "No I don't."

"Then let's go home."

He sounded impatient, but she didn't care. He was going away soon anyhow. The closeness she felt to Jeff wasn't mutual.

By the time they got home, dinner was on the table and Martin stood at the bar, stirring a pitcher full of martinis. He was wearing the grey and blue striped tie that Sue Ellen had bought him as an extra present on his own charge account. The radio was saying something about Hitler's Luftwaffe, but Martin turned the station to some music as they took off their coats.

Sue Ellen looked around for her mother, knowing that she had to face her sooner or later.

Martin noticed and said, "Your mother's a little under the weather, Susie. She's staying in bed for awhile." His attitude seemed matter-of-fact, yet beneath it Sue Ellen sensed an irritation which was very unlike Martin.

Jeff said, "Everybody has a cold. Half the school has been out this week."

The three of them sat down to dinner. Sue Ellen kept thinking that she should go inside and ask Mother if there was anything she wanted. And yet it was so peaceful. She felt like a rabbit in the moment before its foot gets caught in the hidden trap.

"Maybe she'd like a bowl of soup," she said at last, hoping that Martin would instruct her not to go inside.

"Maybe," he said.

Sue Ellen had no choice now. She got a bed tray from the kitchen and set a bowl of chicken broth with crackers on it. Her jaw was tight with the impending ordeal. A dark knowledge of the kind of person her mother really was lurked on the edge of her consciousness. She didn't want to face this new understanding.

The door to her mother's room was ajar. Sue Ellen wondered if she had been listening to the dinner conversation. She pushed the door open with an elbow and tried to smile.

The cushions were propped up behind her mother's shoulders, forming a wan background for the thin body. Her hair fell in whisps about her shoulders. She wore no make-up. Her lips were thin and dry. Sue Ellen shuddered to see how old she looked.

"I brought you some soup," she said, not knowing what else to say.

Her mother turned her face away so that her cheek rested against the pillow. She sighed and did not try to smile in return. The room smelled close and heavy with cigarette smoke. Sue Ellen approached the bed and started to put the tray across her mother's knees. She wished that the nightgown were better adjusted on the thin shoulders. The straps fell carelessly, exposing too much of the flat chest. It offended Sue Ellen that her mother would let herself go like this. She had always taken so much pride in her appearance. Sue Ellen felt uncomfortable. A wave of something like shame surged through her.

"How do you feel?" she said in a little voice, hoping her mother would respond. Say anything, but break the silence which embarrassed Sue Ellen and made her want to run away.

"Tired. So, so tired." The voice held a tremor.

"Maybe we should call the doctor?" She stood helplessly with the tray. Her mother had made no move to accept it.

"I don't need a doctor. I need my family to love me."

Sue Ellen didn't know what to answer. The word love was something her mother seldom mentioned. It was a word that touched on forbidden territory. Love. Love was what you saw in the movies. It was warm and tender and natural. On her mother's lips, the word love was a hideous thing.

"We love you," Sue Ellen offered, knowing in her heart that she was not speaking the truth. She never could imagine loving her mother. At least not the way she remembered loving Daddy. Mother was something she took for granted. A necessary evil who pointed out all the weak spots, all the failings. Mother kept you on guard.

"You'd better go back to Martin," her mother said. It was a bitter command.

Perplexed and tense, Sue Ellen set the tray on the dressing table and fled from the room.

Martin looked at her questioningly as Sue Ellen flung herself on the sofa, her breath coming hard as though she had run uphill.

"Supposing I take you kids to the movies tonight," he said.

Movies had a special meaning for Sue Ellen and involuntarily her face flushed. She glanced quickly at Jeff.

Jeff said, "I've got too much homework."

"Well," Martin said, "that leaves you and me, Susie."

"Fine," Sue Ellen replied with more enthusiasm than she realized.

It was the Christmas season. There were many shows to see, festivities to enjoy. Sue Ellen's mother preferred to remain in bed. The doctor came and pronounced that there was nothing organically wrong with her. She was just tired. He prescribed a tonic. Martin tried to play nursemaid but she rebuffed his advances as she had Sue Ellen's. Jeff remained engrossed with his studies. So Martin began buying tickets for just Sue Ellen and himself.

For Christmas Martin bought Sue Ellen her first coat with a mink collar. On New Year's Eve he took her to a penthouse restaurant where they could watch the crowds without being jostled by them. Sue Ellen began to prize the way he treated her like a real lady. Because she wanted to be worthy of this attention, she began to avoid being alone with Jeff. At least she wanted to avoid him.

But there were repercussions from the sexual experiences she had had. She would go to bed at night and dream of men and women together. And when she awoke her body was a mass of nerves that made her restless. The problem of being just a little beyond twelve years old became a huge obstacle. Neither woman nor child, Sue Ellen seemed to dangle in the center of a chasm. She knew it wasn't nice to think the thoughts which obsessed her. And yet she couldn't revert to believing in Santa Claus with all the naive innocence that had been so easy. Her body cried for caresses but she still had to wear loafers and bobby socks. Sometimes she would be sitting in the kitchen with a glass of milk and chocolate chip cookies when the pulsing, beating rhythm would start in the lower part of her belly. Sometimes this feeling caught her unaware during an examination in school or when she was taking a bath. She kept remembering the feel of Jeff's hand against her. She needed something. She needed somebody. And so she would seek Jeff out and force him away from his studies. After such a time she could forget her body for awhile and be a good daughter to Martin. Her greatest ambition, she believed, was to become his best friend.

With the coming of spring her mother consented to an exploratory stroll on the avenue. She hadn't been out of the house since the turn of the year. Sue Ellen wanted to accompany her. But she looked at her daughter's creamy complexion, the newly voluptuous curve of her hips and turned from Sue Ellen in disgust.

They rarely spoke to each other now. But Sue Ellen began to feel pity in place of the old fear. She looked at her mother and saw a withered leaf waiting to curl up and die. She looked at Martin and saw a man suddenly alone with himself, bewildered and sad. Sue Ellen's compassion was totally for Martin. The memory of her mother pleading with him that night burned in her ears, though now she rarely heard a word exchanged between them after the lights were out. She realized, without consciously thinking so, that her mother had given up sex forever.

The idea of living out the rest of one's days unsated struck Sue Ellen with a quick terror. Now it was April. New green buds gave the air a countrylike freshness. She felt the blood coursing through her own body like sap in a strong young tree. But Jeff would be gone soon. No more Jeff. No more…

CHAPTER FIVE

"I felt trapped. Caged. Choking. My whole life seemed to depend on being able to have a man if I needed one."

Dr. Ross remained silent, waiting for her to continue.

"I tried not to think about what it would be like to touch Martin. Mother didn't sleep with him any more. Ever. I knew it because I used to listen for any sound of that kind. Poor Martin. He must have been suffering the same way I was. More than anything else, it was a feeling of being deserted that we shared. I hated mother for torturing him like that. But what could I do to help him? The idea of kissing him on the lips, just once, plagued me. I was afraid. I was afraid that he would think I was just like Mother."

"What do you mean, just like mother?"

"A sex fiend." Sue Ellen burst out laughing. "Funny. Me worrying about that. Preview of coming attractions, I guess."

"Let's get back to why you think your mother was a sex fiend."

"Well, it seemed more than obvious to me. Martin had stopped being able to satisfy her, she thought. And she was too moral to go out and have affairs with other men. So I suppose she just decided to give up. That's why she stayed in bed. A kind of living death. Without sex, there was nothing in life to live for. Oh, she couldn't admit this to herself, consciously. But any outsider looking at the circumstances would come to the same conclusion."

"Why do you say your mother only *thought* that Martin couldn't satisfy her?"

"I'm coming to that. It was my sweet sixteen party..."

Even though her mother insisted she wasn't up to the fuss and bother, Martin said that his only daughter deserved a commemoration of her most important birthday. They had both become accustomed to the weak voiced complaints and it did not intimidate them.

There was little that could intimidate Sue Ellen anyway. She was the star of the household. Tall like her father, she had his robustness also. At sixteen she looked a healthy twenty. Her hair retained its natural silver blondness and she combed it in a soft wave of bangs over her high, imperious forehead. She had learned the valuable lesson of carrying her body erect. The thrust of her breasts caught many a man's eye and she was proud of it. Her mother could no longer deny Sue Ellen the privilege of mascara and lipstick. And she used them well, accenting the lashes of her green eyes to make them stormy, outlining the willful curve of her lips with fire red. She could have had many boy friends from her class. But they were like children to her. Even Jeff, whom she saw during college vacations, seemed to be getting younger. He was certainly no longer the man she wanted to possess with the full promise of her being.

But tonight promised Sue Ellen a special chance to flaunt herself and she was happy to take advantage of it. Martin had hired caterers. The living room walls were lined with buffets of caviar, smoked turkey, sliced ham and dozens of exotic delicacies which had French names and tasted delicious. Champagne stood waiting in buckets of ice. The room was alive with light, Sue Ellen brighter than all New York in an ice blue dress sprinkled with sequins which molded her breasts, hips, the long line of her thighs. And Martin, older but beaming, surveyed his possession.

They waited for the arrival of the first guests while Sue Ellen's mother decided, before her own mirror, whether or not she must make an appearance.

Around eight o'clock Sue Ellen's friends began to arrive. Mothers and daughters in matching fur coats embraced Sue Ellen and exclaimed over her dress. Jeff shook hands, hitched at the bow tie of his dinner suit and helped his father ladle punch for the young ladies and pour cocktails for their parents. The room filled with the sound of happy chatter and the clinking of glasses. Whiskey mixed its odor with the various perfumes emanating from behind soft earlobes and smooth wrists.

Chipper and Paul, no longer annoyed at the nuisance of Sue Ellen's company, each kissed her congratulations with the bud of ardent desire. Amused Sue Ellen recalled their first meeting at the beach. How well she knew by the points of light in their eyes that she was no longer a pain.

She picked up a cigarette and a flame came around her shoulder to light it. Sue Ellen turned.

"Oh, Richard," she exclaimed. "I didn't see you come in."

"No," he smiled. "You were rather busy." He wore his dark hair combed straight back from the widows peak of his angular face. The years had added muscle to the breadth of his shoulders. But more than that, Sue Ellen noticed the clean curves of his fingernails. She had a thing about hands. Hands were precious to her. They were the paths which opened up roads and detours of pleasure. Only clean, well-kept fingers could make her respond. She studied Richard's fingers and the blue stone of his ring.

"I'm so glad you could come," she said, forgetting for the moment that there were other guests to greet.

"Do you think I would have missed this?" His smile was gentle and friendly. His eyes did not move with insinuation along the frame of her body. And yet Sue Ellen felt something intangible touch between them. It surprised her.

Before she could answer his question, a cluster of girls swept Sue Ellen into other conversation. Some were in pink tulle, others in green or yellow chiffon. All had milk white smiles and the right amount of sophistication for their age. Sue Ellen stood alone in sleekness.

She was tasting a bit of liver pate when she felt the touch of a hand on her elbow. Without looking, she knew the familiar width of Martin's palm.

"Having a good time, honey?" The smell of alcohol on his breath was warm and sweet. That was the thing she liked best about Martin's person. Whiskey went stale on other men. But with Martin, it was always a pleasant comforting odor, like the familiarity of her own linen.

"Wonderful, darling," she answered and took his glass to sip from.

When she started to hand it back to him, he said, "Keep it. I'll get myself another."

"All right." The bubbly taste was new and different for Sue Ellen. She had never cared for the sting of martinis or Scotch and water. But champagne had a funny sparkle. Still sipping from the glass, she danced a few bars of a fox trot with Jeff. He seemed disgruntled about something but she didn't care. This was her night, after all. And Jeff had no right to spoil it with his own problems. Chipper cut in and held her very close. She could see the little dents on either side of his nose from the glasses that he probably wore all day.

"If you're not doing anything," Chipper said, "supposing we go out on the town Friday. You know, for old time's sake."

I'll bet, Sue Ellen thought. She could feel the muscles of his belly rubbing against her. But Chipper himself didn't excite her at all. The champagne, her special evening, the approval of all her guests made Sue Ellen's nerves susceptible to any stimulation. She excused herself from Chipper's tight grip and went to put her glass down.

Martin stopped her hand. He had just finished pouring for three mothers and a father. The bottle was still in his hand.

"Hold it up," he said to her.

And as usual Sue Ellen obeyed him. She listened to the burbling sound as the glass filled up. Then Martin poured more for himself. His blue eyes had a film of happy unreality over them. The line of his jaw, a little too heavy from years of drinking alone and keeping his troubles to himself, was a little firmer tonight. She knew that Martin was enjoying this evening, as though she were his real daughter. She reached up and kissed him beside the ear.

"Thank you," she whispered.

"Oh oh." Martin's arm tensed and she turned to follow the line of his vision.

Standing at the entrance to the living room was Sue Ellen's mother. She had put on a peach colored dress of silk which had been her favorite six or seven years ago. It had fit her tightly then, but she had lost weight from her too thin frame. The dress sagged between her breasts, which, too obviously, were not held by a brassiere. A row of buttons down the front were improperly closed. Gaps showed naked skin. Sue Ellen stared in horror.

She put her trembling hand high up along the door frame and made the semblance of a deep bow.

"Good evening, ladies and gentlemen," she said in a voice that fluttered.

The room became stilled in a shock of silence. All eyes stared fascinated at the caricature of a face. It had heavy penciled eyebrows looming above a perfectly white nose powdered with old fashioned corn starch. Twin circles of rouge were like targets in the hollow cheeks. And the mouth was a tremendous smear of color in no conceivably natural shape.

Sue Ellen broke away from Martin and ran to her mother. She dragged her backward into the room and shut the door. A little giggle rose from the woman's lips as she fell onto the bed and bounced there limply.

"I'm beautiful," she trilled. "I am so beautiful that even my own daughter is jealous of me. My flesh and blood. Men, men.

Men are wicked beasts who make a woman crawl. Don't you love them, Sue Ellen. They're cold, wicked creatures. All they want is to …. See! There's a man crawling under my bed now." She rolled herself up into a ball. Clutching her knees, she giggled wildly.

Afraid to leave her alone, afraid to stay, Sue Ellen could only wait for Martin to join her. At last he came in.

They stood looking at each other as Sue Ellen's mother continued to point out men climbing in her window, hiding in the closet.

Martin lifted the telephone extension and called a hospital.

"You'd better go outside and attend to your guests," he said to her.

"Yes."

With head proudly high Sue Ellen returned to the living room. She knew instinctively that her mother's voice had carried. And what they hadn't heard, their troubled faces surmised. One by one, they excused themselves.

Richard was the last to go. He took her hands between his warm ones. "When everything is settled, I hope we can see each other?"

She would have been glad, except that her mind was still in the bedroom. "Of course," she said absently.

Jeff took Richard to the door. Then they faced each other in the bare living room. Ash trays filled with the long butts of cigarettes, half emptied plates of food, glasses all stood in silent gaudy desolation.

"It was bound to," Jeff said. He put his hand on Sue Ellen's shoulder. "I hope you're not blaming yourself."

Sue Ellen felt dry and hollow. "Poor Daddy," she murmured. She was thinking of a red haired man in Virginia.

Within the hour her mother had been taken away for observation. Martin came back into the living room and sat down in his reading chair. He opened his tie and stared off far away some place.

Jeff said, "Maybe I'd better start cleaning up this mess." With an armload of dishes, he escaped through the swinging doors into the kitchen.

"Come here," Martin said in a flat voice.

Sue Ellen came over. She pulled up an extra chair and sat down beside him.

"She'll be getting the proper attention now," he said. "All these years. I should have known. Should have done something."

Sue Ellen put her hand on his knee. He looked very young to her with his eyes wide and introspective. She wanted to sit on his lap again. Pretend it was long ago and everything fine. But it had never been fine between Martin and her mother. She realized that now. All those years of torture for Martin alone with her mother in that bedroom.

"Don't blame yourself," she said gently. "You were wonderful. You still are."

He looked at her. "Am I?"

"Yes. Truly." She didn't know how to prove it to him. But she needed desperately to convince him of this. Hardly thinking about the consequence of her action, she leaned forward and kissed him on the lips.

Something flamed. Martin leaned the weight of his body forward. His arms went around Sue Ellen's waist. Her lips parted. She pressed herself against his chest.

They broke apart and stared at each other with new understanding. Sue Ellen knew that he would be waiting for her tonight after Jeff went to sleep.

Perversely she and Martin avoided looking at each other while they went about the business of carrying dishes and trays and glasses to the kitchen. But Martin's presence was a part of Sue Ellen with every step she took. Jeff, pensive and concerned, seemed to be doing everything he could to avoid sleep. Sue Ellen felt annoyed with him but dared not show it.

An eternity crawled by before he went off to his own room. Quickly then, Sue Ellen retired to hers. She got into the shower and washed with special care. She leaned against the tile, letting the stream of water bounce against her nipples. Her heart galloped uncontrollably but her arms moved with almost slow motion as she lathered her back and legs and arms. Delicate even to her own touch, her skin seemed a web of little nerve endings. The word virgin fled in and out of her mind. Tales of blood on the sheet, legends of pain were all meaningless. She could conceive of nothing but a whirlpool of pleasure in Martin's bed.

When she had dried herself and dusted Lilac powder over belly and chest, she listened for the sound of Jeff's breathing. Minutes she waited until it came to her ears, steady in monotonous, sleepful rhythm. Quickly she tiptoed back into her room and slipped into a bathrobe. She regretted that Martin had never bought her a negligee. But why should he have?

Her hot palm found the cold glass knob of the door. She turned it and heard the latch click. A bit of moonlight filtered in and she could see Martin's bare chest above the sheet. His bed looked large and empty and waiting. She went to it and sat down on the edge of the mattress.

"Don't be afraid," Martin whispered. He put his hand behind her head and brought her willing lips down to his. The bathrobe spread open. She came down on her stomach beside him, feeling the cool sheet on her legs. His fingers undid the sash of her robe and then he pushed it backward from her shoulders.

His lips found the hollow of her throat as the soft material of her robe folded to the floor.

"Oh, Martin."

She was lying beside him now, one leg in between his. The broad palms which had touched an elbow, escorted her to the best places, helped her into a cab, now moved down between her shoulder blades. She shuddered. The expectation of fulfillment overwhelmed her. This was what she had been dreaming about, it seemed, for almost all of her life. The touch of a man. The brave, uninhibited searching of body for body. She pressed herself against his side, feeling his fingers caress the soft flesh of her hips.

Sue Ellen wanted to wait for him to guide her. But her body knew its own pathway. She lifted herself and lay flat on top of him, feeling her moist breasts flattening against his chest. Her body began to move against his. The breath caught in thick sobs in her throat. Her hands went into his hair and clutched.

"Don't be afraid," he whispered. "I won't hurt you."

"I'm not."

What he had taken for fear was simple eagerness. Yet she hesitated to have him think her a wanton. Curbing her desire, she lay still against him.

He turned her onto her back. She pulled him down hard on top of her. A breath of cool air touched the damp undersides of her legs. Her nipples were hard spears of desire as his lips touched one and then the other.

Her fingernails bit into the flesh of his thigh as he reached across to the drawer of the little table beside the bed. With forced patience she waited until he was ready.

Her hips were already in motion as he approached her. She could not tell pain from ecstasy. Her arms clamped tight around him, held fast as though she were lunging with the last breath of her desire.

She pressed herself so tightly upward that she was off the bed.

Then she sank back, putting her lips gently against Martin's forehead.

"You know," he said after awhile, "it's unusual…"

She put her finger across his lips. "Don't say it," she murmured. "Don't say anything, just lie here."

CHAPTER SIX

"We could hardly wait for Jeff to go back to school."

The abstract painting seemed to nod and bend toward Sue Ellen. She had become accustomed to the sound of Dr. Ross's pen as he made notes on the large yellow paper.

"First I had been hiding from Martin with Jeff. Now I was hiding from Jeff with Martin. It amused me even then. Of course I wanted to think about anything except my mother and where she was. Sex with Martin was the best outlet. I became a woman with him. That night ended my childhood forever."

"Childhood is not so easily defined as that. When you say childhood, what do you think of?"

"Innocence."

"But you weren't exactly innocent with Jeff."

"That was different. I mean it was play. We were toys for each other. Rubbing and tickling. But it isn't the same thing as deep intercourse. It certainly could not satisfy me the same way. There just isn't any comparison. Martin knew what he was doing. He wasn't afraid and he taught me how to relax in bed. Sometimes we would stay in bed all day. Like some people stay in bars all day, I suppose."

"Why do you make that comparison?" A ray of sun prismed off Dr. Ross's glasses and made a little rainbow on the wall.

"When I think of alcohol, I think of people escaping from their troubles. When I remember going to bed with Martin, I get the same feeling. We loved each other in a way. A desperate way. Neither of us ever mentioned mother yet it hung between us after we were satisfied. I could almost smell the fluffy odor of her cosmetics in the bed as we lay still and listened to the far off sound of the traffic below."

"What about your mother?"

"I never can get away from her. I couldn't then and I can't seem to now. She follows me as though I were the guilty one. As though I were responsible for what happened to her."

"You can hate her if you want to. It's not against the law."

Sue Ellen closed her eyes tight, feeling the old trip hammer of anxiety beating at the wall around her heart.

"But I don't hate her. And I don't want to hate her. I just want to forget her sometimes. She's like a Siamese twin."

She heard the sound of Dr. Ross's breathing. It was a quiet steadying sound. "Well, perhaps now you will begin to understand a little bit deeper into your problem. Nymphomania is a flight through sex. When a person cannot face his relationships and see them squarely, he can do a number of things to evade the issue. A hyper-sex life is one solution."

"Don't tell me that my mother is responsible for my behavior."

"I'm not telling you anything. You're telling me, remember? But you won't be able to resolve your difficulties until you stop long enough to consider just how you did respond to your mother and what it meant to you."

Sue Ellen paused. "All I can do is feel sorry for her. She always wanted more than she could get. Of everything. Martin should have made her happy. He tried. Lord knows how he tried."

"Did he make you happy?"

"For awhile, yes. But I began to want too much also. When I found out how apparently simple it was to avoid becoming pregnant, my interests widened. And, of all things, I began to be obsessed with a desire to go to Virginia and find my real father. The more I went to bed with Martin, the more I thought of him as a stranger. And I began getting lonesome again. He seemed to understand. And so I got my trip."

The train ride which had seemed so long going North seemed even longer on Sue Ellen's return. As she had stared out the window then, not daring to think what she might find at the end of her journey, so she felt now. She listened to the wheels racing over the rails and tried to tell herself not to expect her father to resemble her memory of him. She knew that he would not recognize her, of course. She had nothing in common with the little girl pulled along by her mother ten years ago. Nothing in common except fear.

A small valise lay on the rack over her head. She had decided against taking along too many clothes. Underneath her sensible exterior, she felt a niggling urge not to return to New York. A childish desire, without reason, grounded in unreality, it nevertheless gave Sue Ellen trouble. For no matter what she told herself to the contrary, she could not believe that the little house would look different, that her father would be older and probably unconcerned. She even imagined Clellie still standing on the lawn shouting for Sue Ellen to come inside.

She lit a cigarette and opened the pocket novel sitting on her lap. The words raced before her eyes, unread, unintelligible. Her mind skidded among her troubled thoughts.

For three hours she remained in her seat. Then the sun dipped, a violet horizon made all seem peaceful and finally an unfathomable blackness dotted here and there with lights was all that she could see.

Sue Ellen put down the book and made her way along the aisle from car to car until she reached the club car. Her seventeenth birthday was still some months off but she knew that no bartender would question her age. All she wanted was a few drinks to make her sleep through the night.

Half a dozen people were seated with their drinks but Sue Ellen noticed only the soldier leaning with his elbows on the bar, his overseas cap tilted back from the sandy colored crew cut. What impressed her was the curving angle of his body. It had a feeling of desolation, of apartness which made Sue Ellen respond though she could not see his face. She went up beside him and placed herself on a stool. From this position she could see his profile. A young face, weatherbeaten by who knew what horrible experiences. His corporal's chevrons pointed to service stars on the pocket of his Eisenhower jacket.

The bartender put down the towel he was using to polish glasses and said, "What'll it be, Miss?"

She didn't know the names of many drinks nor did she like the taste of most of them.

"A champagne cocktail, please."

The bartender smiled and shook his balding head. "Sorry," he grinned. "The war may be over, but life's still hard. We don't expect champagne on this trip for who knows how long yet. What else can I do you for?"

Sue Ellen was at a loss. She glanced along at the soldier's glass. "What's he drinking?"

"Seagram's seven and seven."

"All right."

She had hoped the soldier would look up and acknowledge her notice of him. But he was concentrating on something else. He hadn't even heard her.

The bartender poured and stirred for her. He was looking at the polish on her nails. "Yep, the war is over," he breathed.

Now the soldier looked up. He had thick bleached eyebrows that contrasted with the dark skinned forehead. "You keep sayin' that. Why do you keep sayin' that?" His voice was a little thick but the amber eyes were still clear. He seemed like he would remain just the other side of sober for the rest of his life.

"Well, it is, isn't it?" the bartender replied amiably.

"Yeah, buddy. I guess it is."

Sue Ellen didn't know why she was partaking of the corporal's unhappiness. Certainly, she had not been touched by the war. Martin's import-export business was something she knew little about. But apparently he had continued to do well, war or no war. Still she could feel something of how it must have been. The newsreels, the headlines. They had given spoiled Americans an inkling.

"Everybody thinks the war is over," the corporal repeated. He turned toward Sue Ellen and his elbow slipped slightly on the counter. "You too, huh?"

"I don't know," she murmured, not wanting to antagonize him. She thought it better not to commit herself in case he had a metal plate in his skull or something else terrible.

"Come on, Delilah, say that the war is over."

"My name's not Delilah." She picked up the glass now and took a sip. It didn't taste so bad. Rather sweet from the Seven-Up.

"Francine. Geraldine. Eileen. You're all Delilah anyway." He touched his glass against the green soda bottle and the bartender set him up another round.

It occurred to Sue Ellen how lucky Jeff had been. ROTC at college. A little marching. Nothing more.

"A woman's place," the soldier continued, "is not at home. Women belong on the front line so they won't go crazy sending salamis to their boys in the service." He sighed and recollected himself. "I'm a bore, aren't I?"

"No," Sue Ellen said simply. As a matter of fact she wanted him to go on. There was a fascination for her in his unhappiness. She had spent time with lots of uniformed men. But they had always been rip-roaring for fun. Out to get a feel, laughs, kicks. Maybe all of them were hiding what this soldier was saying.

"I'll stop now," he said. "Let's talk about you."

Of all things, Sue Ellen did not want to talk about herself. She wished they were sitting in the leather chairs near the window.

Her legs felt uncomfortable perched on the rim of the stool. "I'm not interesting," she said.

"Sure you are. You and me and little ol' ruptured duck, here." He touched the discharge pin in his lapel. "I'm sure you have a very interesting history." He noticed Sue Ellen glancing toward the window seats. "Come on," he said. "We'll go and be private so you can tell me all about it."

"All right," she said, knowing that she could get him to talk about himself very soon. And then she wouldn't have to dwell on what was waiting for her in Virginia.

She was right. The soldier began telling her all about how it was. He remembered a little German girl who used to run between the bombs, her kitten poking his head out of her open hand bag. The more he spoke, the more Sue Ellen realized that her father wasn't going to look the same at all. Not at all.

The train raced through the night. She should have been in bed by now.

He told her he was going to Florida. He was very drunk now but Sue Ellen, because she was on her fourth drink, didn't realize this. Her head was dancing in a funny circle that made her feel very adventurous. She began to think that her father probably wasn't even in Virginia any more. She felt cut loose from the whole world. She felt that she wanted to be in bed, but not alone. Never alone again for as long as she lived.

The bartender started turning off the lights.

"We're getting kicked out," the soldier said.

His voice suffused her with a tinny feeling of not being real. She could have been a toy soldier, like him, sitting alone, forgotten beneath the Christmas tree.

"I'm not sleepy," she said.

She was never going to be sleepy again. Not until she was married, anyway.

"Okay," he said. "We can go for a walk through the train."

Sue Ellen climbed unsteadily to her feet. The rocking motion of the train made walking even more difficult. They stopped in the shadows of the vestibule. The soldier crumpled an empty cigarette package and stuffed it back into his pocket. Then he leaned his hand against the wall beside her shoulder.

"You're a nice girl, Delilah."

"Not Delilah."

His face was very close to her own. She tried not to look into his probing eyes, but she could not avoid them. Something about them seemed to be reaching out for her. They were strangers and yet she might have known him all her life. Each had wandered the earth, wanting to be found, wanting to be taken. And each had found useless destruction. Sue Ellen touched her lips lightly to his. They stood close as the train ran its course southward.

They spent the few remaining hours until morning together in a world which had neither beginning nor end. The quality of travel made it like a suspended moment in life. Responsibility released its claim from Sue Ellen. She began to wonder if it were wise for her to seek her father after all these years. After all the letters she had written which had gone unanswered.

"Norfolk. Next stop, Nor—folk."

They were seated now, their shoulders barely touching. She looked down at his hands with the fingers spread helplessly on the crease of his trousers. Good strong hands that had held a gun. That could hold a woman. A quick breath escaped from Sue Ellen's lips. It felt like a dove rushing to freedom. She sat very still. The train began to move again, irrevocably toward Florida.

"Well now," the corporal said.

She hadn't told him that Norfolk was her stop. She could settle with the conductor the next time he came around. For all she knew the corporal was going home to a wife and children. But it didn't matter. This moment alone. A second in time with someone who felt the same needs she felt. Even if he got off the train and ran to another woman's arms, it would have been worth the trip.

When the train pulled into Miami, Sue Ellen waited but there was no one to greet him. She stood on the platform with her valise and he saw her waiting.

"Can I give you a lift?" he said.

"Sure. Where are you going?" the dustless air picked out a tone of vivacity in her voice.

"Collins and Lincoln. My sister has a jewelry store. I guess I'll find her there if anyplace." He lifted the duffle bag and whistled for a taxi.

As they rode along Sue Ellen looked at the palm trees casually. She didn't feel casual. The dry heat made her feel like taking off her clothes. A cold bath would be good. Her girdle felt too restricting, especially in contrast with the girls who strolled along the streets in shorts.

"You can take me to a hotel," Sue Ellen said.

"Which?"

"Anyone."

"Hey now, you can't do that." He was looking at her with concern. "This is the middle of the season. You have to have a reservation round these parts."

"Oh." She wasn't frightened or concerned about being left on the street. The corporal was too interested. He would take care of her.

"My sister'll think of something," he said. "You know how the natives are."

She didn't know anything, except that her destiny was to be with this corporal. At least for a night. The trip had fatigued her. The muscles in her back felt sore from all the sitting and standing. Her lips felt dry. No doubt she had eaten off the lipstick. She took a compact out of her purse and considered the uncombed hair that fell wildly about her shoulders. With a slow movement of her hand, she lifted the weight of hair off her neck and felt a breeze touch her skin.

The taxi stopped on the crowded thoroughfare and Sue Ellen stepped out. She could smell the ocean which lay just beyond a tall Spanish type hotel pinkly bright against the crystal blue sky.

"Come on." The corporal took her valise and his duffle bag and headed for a store with large costume pieces glittering in both windows.

Sue Ellen waited in the doorway as a young woman rushed out from behind the counter and flung herself into the corporal's arms.

"Frank! Frank! Why didn't you call? I'd have met you." The woman's interest was suddenly cut short as she noticed Sue Ellen waiting.

Their eyes met and Sue Ellen thought she was looking at Frank's twin. The woman's sandy colored hair was just a little bit longer than her brother's and she wore it brushed back from her temples. She wore little pearl earrings which softened only faintly the angles of her face. One neat eyebrow, well plucked but unpenciled, rose ever so slightly. She disengaged herself from her brother.

Sue Ellen watched her approach. The compact body displayed small but rounded breasts and emphasized the trimness of hips which swayed slightly in her white suit. Her navy shoes had very high heels, bringing her to an inch above Sue Ellen's height.

"May I help you?" she said in a controlled voice very different from the greeting she had given Frank.

Sue Ellen knew that this woman knew she wasn't a customer. It was a strange approach from a woman, Sue Ellen thought. But it pleased her.

"Oh, that's my travelling mate," Frank interjected. "She came all the way from New York without reservations. I said you could help her find something."

"Perhaps I can," the woman said. She held out a hand with a dazzling turquoise on the ring finger. "I'm Julia Bennett."

"Your brother calls me Delilah," she laughed nervously, not understanding why she felt ill at ease. "Sue Ellen's my real name. Sue Ellen Gaynor." The fact that a woman could be taller than herself impressed Sue Ellen.

"Well, how about it, Julia? Know of a pigeon roost for the wandering pigeon?" Frank came up and put his arm around his sister's shoulder. It didn't belong there on the spotless jacket, but Frank seemed oblivious in this moment of reunion.

"Sue Ellen can stay with us," she said, "until we find something more to her taste." Then, looking directly at Sue Ellen, she added, "It will be no inconvenience."

Sue Ellen's glance dropped to the ruffle of Julia's white blouse. She knew just the type of body beneath it. A mild curiosity filled her to discover if her conjecture was correct. "Thank you," she said.

"Take Sue Ellen home now and the two of you freshen up a bit. I'll be along about six."

"Right-o," Frank said. "You're a doll. Come on, Delilah. We could both use a good bath."

"Use my car," Julia called after them. "It's across the street."

Frank tossed their things into the back of a white Mercedes sports coupe. Sue Ellen arranged herself against the black leather seat, thinking that Julia certainly knew her own personality and tastes. It was definitely something to know who you were, she decided. Frank opened the glove compartment and took out the keys. He eased into traffic. A breeze drifted lightly against her cheeks, lulling her into a need for sleep. It felt like years since she had stretched out on a bed. Frank's continuing chatter sounded like a distant buzz in her ears. But she appreciated his efforts to be cheerful and exuberant.

They drove out from the center of town and past stucco houses in pastels of green and blue and pink. Martin had often wanted for the family to come here for a vacation. Only Mother detested the South. She didn't want to recall those awful years, she said. But Miami was certainly different from Virginia. People here looked well fed and well rested and out for a good time.

Sue Ellen felt the car stop.

"That's ever-lovin' home," Frank said.

She saw a well-trimmed garden lush with elephant ear, a pineapple shaped tree, a statue of some Greek god. Behind it the white single storied house which completed the picture of Julia and her Mercedes.

Inside past the oak polished door lay a high ceilinged expanse of rooms, cooled in atmosphere by a cross section of beams underneath the pitched roof. All the furnishings contrived for comfort and leisure. Teakwood chairs laced with rattan blended elegantly with the gold and green hangings between two windows. The lush side of Julia, Sue Ellen thought, which she kept out of her shop and her business.

But though she was curious, her mind refused to remain astute. Frank showed her where the bathroom was, gave her a terrycloth robe and left her in privacy.

Slowly she undid the hooks of her dress and let it fall to the blue tiling. She reached painfully back and loosened the fastenings of her bra. Heavily her breasts slipped down, red lines of constriction criss-crossing the tender flesh low beneath her nipples. She put her palms on them and massaged delicately. Thoughtless of time, she stood thus, feeling the flesh bulge and swell and roll. She sighed and reached to pull off her girdle.

A knock at the door stopped her. "You okay?" Frank's voice had something in it more than hospitable curiosity.

She reached over and turned the door handle. "I'm fine," she said, looking up at him from her nakedness.

He swallowed and stepped toward her. She thought, fleetingly: he's a stranger. But the thought had no meaning. Frank was a man. All good things.

"We can bathe together," she suggested, turning on the faucets.

Before he could answer, she began unbuttoning his shirt. The sensation of male flesh to her touch thrust aside all drowsiness. But she wanted to tease herself. Prolong the delicious expectation. She looked at Frank devouringly. A surge of need swept away playfulness. She dragged him down on the floor and pulled him against her.

In the wildness of their motions Sue Ellen banged her arm against a chrome leg of the wash basin. It did not matter. They clung and rolled desperately. It was as though a bomb might explode over their heads any moment.

"Oh, please do it," she rasped. "Please." She wiggled beneath him, trying to adjust her position. She flung one leg up against the wall. The shower water splashed drops out onto them.

"Not yet," he said. "I need you to …"

Sue Ellen knew what he wanted, but it was something she had never tried before. And for a moment she hesitated, afraid to trust herself.

"Go on," he whispered hoarsely.

She threw herself upon him, her temples throbbing insensibly. She became wild, uncaring.

She felt Frank relax with a sudden deflation of his whole body.

"Well, Delilah," he smiled. "The war is over."

But the war wasn't over yet. At least not for her. He looked at his watch. "My God. It's five of six." He patted her left breast. "Gosh, kid. I didn't mean to hang you up like this. But Julia …"

Sue Ellen gritted her teeth. "Get out!" she yelled. "Get out!"

Frank picked up his clothes and left the bathroom.

Trembling she tried to stand up. Her body was a film of perspiration that ran in rivulets down her spine. She crawled into the shower and sat there on the floor letting the water beat at her. There was no way she could get through the rest of the evening like a human being with this demon driving inside her. Sitting cross-legged, she stared down at herself. The saliva felt full in her mouth.

She hated herself desperately. Then she pulled her thighs tight together, trying to squash the throbbing, pulsing need. No use.

Somewhere she had read in a book about women alone. Boys did it all the time, she knew. But it was a simple matter for boys. The idea of herself alone this way held a terror of dissatisfaction. Yet gradually she began to experiment. Anything would be better than nothing.

Satisfaction came quickly and easily. All too easily. It did not fulfill her real need. One salted peanut. She laughed bitterly.

Afterward she gave herself up to the torment of cold water, hoping that the icy sensation would quiet her and take her mind off her body.

She stepped out and towelled herself dry and put on the terrycloth robe. It gave off a faint fragrance of sandalwood. Julia's perfume, no doubt. A brisk and unruffled odor, which hinted at something Sue Ellen could not quite define. Her hair hung in damp strands about her face but she knew better than to look for pins in Julia's cabinet.

Folding her clothes neatly under one arm, she stepped barefoot out of the bathroom. The pungent aroma of good coffee floated in from someplace.

"Frank?" she called, wanting him to show her to her bedroom. More than anything, she needed a good cry.

The sound of clicking heels drew closer. Julia stepped around the corner. Her jacket was off now and so was the ruffled blouse. In their place she wore a pale green polo shirt of a tissue knit material which showed off the flatness of her stomach.

"Frank's pooped out," she said. There was no hint in her voice of anything which accused. Her amber eyes were a deep yellow, reflecting the shirt. "You're dogged too, of course. Would you like some coffee before you turn in?"

Sue Ellen shook her head. She wanted to be alone to get hold of herself. Surely this woman would see if she stayed much longer in her presence.

"All right then, come with me."

Meekly Sue Ellen followed the well-shaped calves along a parquet floor to a room which overlooked the back garden. From the window she could see a bird bath glittering in the final rays of sunlight.

"Pajamas might be in order," Julia said. "I'm sure mine will fit you." She inspected the girl's body with an appraising eye.

"I have some in my suitcase," Sue Ellen offered shakily.

"You don't want to bother with that now," she said.

Julia opened a drawer and lifted out a pair of blue silk pajamas. "Try these."

Without thinking Sue Ellen took off her robe and reached out for the pajamas. In that instant she caught Julia's gaze fixed hungrily on her breasts.

A childish desire to fling herself on this woman and cry and cry against that neat sweater almost overcame her. She took the pajamas and turned away, afraid that she might make a fool of herself.

"See you when you wake up," Julia said. She went out and closed the door silently behind her.

Sue Ellen didn't bother with the pajamas. She fell down on the bed and waited for the tears to come. But, oddly enough, they didn't. Her body yearned, unsated. But her emotions were somehow quieted. She went to sleep dreaming about Julia and her quiet, smiling voice.

CHAPTER SEVEN

D r. Ross opened the window an inch more from the top. "Had you ever experienced a homosexual relationship before then?"

Sue Ellen thought back to her early teens. "Nothing to speak of," she said. "There was the usual comparing that girls do. I remember once not believing that people had hair in that place. And I challenged the girl who said so to show me."

"Did she?"

"Yes. Nothing happened beyond that, though. I couldn't imagine how two people with the same fixtures could make a go of it. You know the old chestnut, nature abhors a vacuum. Well, women just didn't enter into my range of possibilities. There was nothing attractive to me about breasts. In fact I deplored them until I discovered what an advantage they are with men. Tell me something. Can a man feel a woman having an orgasm?"

"That depends on the woman, doesn't it?"

"I make a terrible racket," Sue Ellen said. "Men seem to like it that way. But women, I still don't know anything about them. You'd think I wasn't one of the club or something. They've always been such strangers to me."

"Was your mother a stranger?" She heard the little snapping sound as he filled the old-fashioned Waterman.

"Definitely."

"You say that you liked Julia's cool efficiency. You wanted to cry on her neat sweater. Does that sound familiar to you?"

"No, should it?"

"What did you say about your mother when you were on your way to New York?"

"I don't remember. Did I say she was cool and efficient looking? It's hard to believe that she was. But I guess that's true, isn't it? Mother was slender and always in control. Yes, so was Julia."

"Any connection now?"

"Vaguely, doctor. Very vaguely. Mother never earned a nickle with her own two hands. Julia had her own business."

She awoke sometime during the middle of the night. The salty tang of surf drifted in to her nostrils. Slowly she recalled what had happened between yesterday and now. Martin. Martin would be expecting her to phone him. Perhaps he was sitting in his wing chair right now, wondering why he hadn't heard from her.

Midst these thoughts of responsibility, Sue Ellen became aware once again of the strange sandalwood fragrance. She reached out and touched the silk pajamas. She drew the yielding material to her cheek. Her naked body felt free and wanton between the sheets. Languidly she put the pajamas on. Their smoothness caressed her skin. And once again she drifted away into a sleep that quivered with unfamiliar emotions.

The sound of knuckles rapping at her door brought Sue Ellen awake into the daylight.

"Hey in there. It's past noon." Frank's voice was eager.

"All right," Sue Ellen answered. "I'll be with you in a minute."

She got out of bed and stretched, feeling oddly at home in this house. Someone had brought her valise in and stood it next to the wicker chair. She took out a shirtwaist dress of amethyst cotton.

Dressed and groomed, she emerged ready and willing for breakfast. Frank stood scrambling eggs in the kitchen. The little table was set for two.

"Drink your orange juice," he said.

She pulled up the chrome-legged chair and started buttering the warm toast.

"Well now," he said. "What would you like to do today? I'm taking a couple of weeks off before going back to the old job. We could have a swell time. Forget the frauleins and all that." He brought over two platefuls of eggs and set one before her. "Maybe you'd like to go water skiing? Get yourself some color on that white skin."

The idea appealed to her and yet it was preposterous. What was she doing here actually? Easter vacation. Frank was looking forward to getting back to work. Julia was certainly very well fixed in her ways. And here she sat, drifting no where. Lazy. Useless.

"Julia'll be home in an hour," he continued. "She's only working half a day today. The three of us'll have a ball."

Instinctively Sue Ellen returned to the one ambition that really possessed her. "You owe me something," she said and watched Frank blush.

"Yeah."

"Well?"

He lifted his shoulders helplessly. "You pick the damndest times."

"I didn't tell you to do it that way."

"All right, all right," he said irritably. "Let's forget it for awhile. There are other things in life, you know."

His words recalled Jeff. There were other things in life, yes. But what? What was she supposed to look forward to? Martin wanted to send her to college. But she wasn't a scholar. The thought of four more years studying about kings and taxation meant nothing to her. She had no pressing need to go out and earn money. Sue Ellen felt very unnecessary in the scheme of things.

"Hey, you don't have to look so morbid," Frank said. "I apologize. I'm sorry. What the hell else do you want?"

"Take it easy," she said. "I wasn't thinking about you at all."

She recalled Julia and how understanding Julia had been the night before. Maybe the woman sensed her waywardness. Maybe she would have something to suggest. A new hope ran through Sue Ellen as she envisioned having a long talk with a woman who could really understand.

They finished breakfast and Sue Ellen did the dishes, waiting alerted for the sound of Julia's heels on the flagstone.

Punctually at one, Julia's car drew up. Sue Ellen heard the motor shut off. Frank was stacking the dishes in the pine cabinet.

"We left you some coffee," he said as Julia came into the kitchen.

"Thanks," she said. "I'll have some." She put her grey purse on the table and sat down. "Hi," she smiled a calm smile at Sue Ellen. "Have a good sleep?"

Sue Ellen watched her unscrew gold earrings from her lobes and drop them into a compartment of the purse. The long angle of her jaw seemed much more prominent without the jewelry, but somehow kinder.

"She just got up an hour ago," Frank interposed. "I'll bet she snores, too."

Sue Ellen, wanting something to do so that she would not expose the mixture of embarrassment and shyness she felt in the woman's presence, poured Julia's coffee.

"Do you take milk and sugar?" Sue Ellen asked, feeling the helplessness of her question.

"Just sugar," Julia answered kindly.

Sue Ellen got the sugar bowl, a teaspoon, a napkin. She wished Frank would go away, knowing that at any second he was going to suggest the water skiing business.

"I thought it would be a good idea," Julia said, "if I took Sue Ellen shopping this afternoon. There's a nice sale on bathing suits."

This was the opening Sue Ellen needed. She took it eagerly. "Yes. I forgot to bring one along."

"What am I going to do, chasing around in women's stores?" Frank said.

"If you want to do me a favor," Julia answered, "why don't you put some oil into the jalousies in the living room. They creak so when I turn them. This place has really gone to pot since you've been away."

"All right," Frank said. "I know when I'm not wanted." A relieved grin softened the tension of his features. No doubt he was worried about what had happened yesterday and here was an opportunity for Sue Ellen to begin forgetting about it.

Julia finished the coffee and reapplied lipstick. "Ready?" she said to Sue Ellen.

"Yes, of course."

The two women got up and left Frank searching in a drawer for the materials with which to fix the windows.

Alone in the sunshine with Julia, Sue Ellen felt a rush of optimism. What she expected, she didn't really know. But the excitement in her body was a joy to feel. At the same time, she prayed that her aloof exterior was sufficient camouflage. Because of her overdeveloped appearance, Sue Ellen was accustomed to being treated like an adult. In many ways she felt and acted more adult than most of the girls in her class. Men were a thrill to her but not an awesome mystery. Sexual knowledge had given her a certain command whereas her friends were still reading books in secret and petting when they felt adventurous. Because she was ahead of them, Sue Ellen had little in common with these girls just growing up. They amused her. But in her heart, she felt like an outsider. Now here she was with a woman who certainly had the advantage of age and even greater experience. Sue Ellen wished that Julia would really talk to her. She desperately needed a friend. And this need made her awkward in conversation. They rode a few blocks down the thoroughfare in complete silence.

"My brother's a good boy," Julia said at last. "He needs to settle down and find himself, but I'm thankful that's all the war did to him."

Sue Ellen realized that Julia had noticed the black and blue mark on her arm. It could have been from anything, she protested inwardly. Did Julia know or was she simply guessing?

"Frank is very good company."

"But you don't want to talk about him. I think you're right." She turned a corner sharply and straightened the wheel. "We'll forget about Frank for the afternoon. Just you...and me." Her voice was satisfied. She touched a strand of hair back into place on her temple. The long fingers came back to rest lightly on the wheel.

There was something which Julia had decided in that instant. It increased Sue Ellen's feeling of closeness to the woman. Nothing further was said, yet their silence now was easier. More intimate.

They pulled up in front of a sportswear shop and went inside. Julia knew the saleslady and called her by her first name. The little woman glanced appraisingly over Sue Ellen and led them into a private fitting room in the back, bringing with her half a dozen bathing suits. Then she pulled the tan curtain closed.

"Call if you need me," she said. The voice came into the little cubicle with a suppressed note of bitterness.

Julia hung the suits on a hook beside the mirror and stood with arms folded as Sue Ellen began to undress. She took the girl's skirt and blouse and slip, placing them on the chair beside both their handbags.

"Well?" Julia said.

Reluctantly Sue Ellen looked at herself in the mirror. She still had on brassiere and panties. Her flesh swelled out in a deep cleavage between the cups of the bra. Nylon panties revealed herself beneath them, but the gossamer covering was better than nothing.

"You're not supposed to try suits on over a naked body," she said with an attempt at matter-of-factness.

"Nonsense. Come along." Julia's fingers beckoned for the underwear.

Sue Ellen had no real reason to object. She certainly wasn't a shy person. And especially in front of another woman, she had even less reason to hesitate. It was childish. Yet she stood there without moving. She stared mutely at Julia.

Julia came up behind her. Efficiently her fingers unsnapped the hooks of Sue Ellen's brassiere. Before she could stop them, Sue Ellen's heavy breasts appeared beneath the emptied satin cups. Julia gazed over Sue Ellen's shoulder at her reflected nakedness in the mirror. As though with a life of their own, the bare nipples hardened into brown pointed circles of flesh. The little dressing room felt very warm, very close.

Afraid that Julia had seen and discovered something about her which Sue Ellen herself didn't know, she quickly slid her panties down off her hips and stood there, daringly naked. The pretense of casualness didn't work. Her breathing became noticeably more shallow and rapid. The smile sat like a mask on her features.

Julia said, "It's all right, baby. It really is." Then she took a bathing suit off the hook and gave it to Sue Ellen.

Thankfully she wiggled into the latex material and drew it up over her hips. It had to be strapped and buttoned down the back. Julia's hands reached out again and fastened the closings. Her palm slid up Sue Ellen's back, apparently by accident.

"Do you like it?" Sue Ellen said in a very little voice.

Julia laughed. "The suit? Yes. I think you could probably wear anything and get away with it. But let's try the others just for comparison."

Sue Ellen felt ill. To go through that agonizing procedure again was more than she could take. But why? Struggling to control her emotions, she pulled off the suit.

Julia handed her the second one, a black wool. But now her eyes travelled leisurely and without guardedness along the curves of the girl's body.

"I didn't realize you were so young," she said in a gentle tone.

Sue Ellen felt a flush roll down the length of her neck. She swallowed and adjusted the black wool straps on her shoulders.

"Oh, the heck with it," Julia blurted suddenly. "We'll take these two. Let's get out of here."

Obediently Sue Ellen took off the second suit. Julia folded the garments over her arm and went out to pay for them, leaving Sue Ellen to dress in privacy.

It was a merciful gesture. Sue Ellen flung her street clothes back onto her body and sat down for a moment to recover herself. She felt, decidedly, that Julia was liking her very much. She couldn't account for it. All that Sue Ellen knew was her own gratefulness.

With the package between them in the car, Sue Ellen leaned back and extracted two cigarettes from her pack.

"Light it for me, will you?" Julia said.

They were racing along beside the ocean. Sue Ellen exhaled the smoke and looked out at the turquoise expanse of glittering water. A violet band encircled the ocean out near the horizon. Brown bodies, reclining in the sand, looked well-greased and content. It was a peacefulness Sue Ellen wished she could experience. Where they were going now, she did not know. And unreasonably, she did not care to know. The whys and the wherefores were so far beyond her that Sue Ellen did not even consider them. She abandoned herself to Julia's wishes, trusting that all would work out for the best.

They drove like this, without speaking, for half an hour. Then Julia pulled the car up in front of a beach house. It was an unpretentious structure of blue clapboard, newly painted and well-kept.

"Home away from home," Julia said.

They went inside and Sue Ellen stood at the window overlooking the ocean. The furniture, made of driftwood, seemed almost part of the ocean itself. It was a good place to hide in, Sue

Ellen thought. A fine place to forget the world. The only place where one could be oneself and not worry about being found out.

"My suit's in the bedroom. You can undress in there."

Sue Ellen took the cardboard box and went into the bathroom. When she came out, Julia was waiting for her. Julia, slim, neatly filling out her own two piece suit, stood with a jar of cocoa butter.

"We'd better rub some of this on you," she suggested.

Without question, Sue Ellen turned and submitted herself to the smooth, plying strokes on her back.

"I'm not so young," she said irrelevantly. "I'm almost eighteen. Martin, he's my step-father, Martin treats me like an adult. It's better to be an adult than try to remain a child all one's life." Her voice swelled and broke as she sought for rational expression.

"Is that what you want, my dear? For me to treat you like an adult?"

Sue Ellen nodded. Beneath the stroking fingers, her mind seemed to come free from all inhibition. Drunk with the sensation of being touched, shivering with the unfulfilled need lying restless since yesterday, she felt driven by her needing. Julia's cool controlling hands subdued all reason. Sue Ellen turned and looked at her questioningly. She didn't know what she was seeking from this woman. But she trusted that Julia had the answer. And the secret of release from her craving. She leaned forward.

"We'd better get into the ocean," Julia said, stepping back.

She took Sue Ellen's hand and dragged her outside.

They ran across the hot sand and dived into the water. It was tepid and calm and languid. Not icy as Sue Ellen knew the northern Atlantic. The sun made diamonds from the drops of water on Julia's arms. Sue Ellen swam close to her. She tried to touch, to grasp the evasive body. But Julia escaped her. She turned and grinned and dove. When she surfaced, Sue Ellen could only splash at her in a weird kind of joyful frustration.

When they came out, Julia sat down in the shade of a tall palm and flung her wet hair back from her forehead. There was no one else on the beach for hundreds of feet. They might as well have been on a desert island. Julia pulled the girl down beside her and made Sue Ellen put her head on her extended legs.

"Tell me more about Martin," she said.

It was easy to talk. Lying thus and staring at the cloudless expanse of blue, Sue Ellen felt no need of secrecy. For more than an hour, the words came from her. And even the stinging pain of her mother flared up and released itself to Julia. She felt the woman's soft touch on her forehead, the fingers going lightly through her hair with an understanding caress. The unsated loneliness in Sue Ellen's heart ebbed a little. A promise of happiness suffused her limbs as she spoke and inhaled the salty odor of Julia's skin.

"Yes," Julia said at last, "in many ways you are an adult."

Sue Ellen reached up and took the woman's hand in her own.

"You'll phone Martin and tell him where you are."

After a while they went back to the beach house and Sue Ellen put the call in immediately. She didn't quite know how to explain her reasons for not getting off in Virginia. But he was happy to hear that she was all right. And in a way, he was glad that she had avoided fulfilling the reckless desire to see her past.

At the end of the call, Sue Ellen felt definitely pleased with herself. "That's much better," she admitted to Julia. "I guess we can get out of these wet suits now."

Free of the skeletons in her closet, Sue Ellen leaned across and undid the one button on Julia's bra top. It was supposed to be an affectionate gesture. Filled with the goodness of her friendship for Julia, she reached up and untied the bow. And now she saw the two firm breasts tilting upward. Their nipples were hard as her own had been. A fury of desire swept Sue Ellen. Blinded by its senseless urging, she fell forward and pressed her lips to one warm breast.

She felt Julia's hand on her neck. Her own arms went around the woman's waist. She pushed her backwards onto the foam rubber couch and pressed her own body on top of her.

"No," Julia said between clenched teeth. "You're just a baby."

The words were cut off by the fury of Sue Ellen's desire. Feverishly she kissed the woman's eyelids, her forehead, down along her ear lobe, the curve of her throat.

"Don't ... don't."

She was deaf to Julia's protests. Her mouth travelled between the breasts into the hollow of the heaving ribs.

And then the wall of Julia's resistance crumbled. She raised herself and embraced Sue Ellen. She turned the girl so that they lay sideways on the couch, their legs intertwined.

Finally Julia unfastened Sue Ellen's bathing suit and slid it down over her trembling body. She got out of the bottom of her own suit. Their bodies, cold from the water, clung tightly. The faintly pungent odor of seaweed enhanced their privacy.

Julia let her hands explore the soft, yielding flesh. A film of perspiration began to warm their meeting bodies. Her fingers trailed down to the quivering thighs.

"Touch me," Sue Ellen moaned.

But the knowing fingers continued to tease. She grabbed Julia's hand and pressed it against her.

Julia's mouth left the moist breasts. Sue Ellen raised herself to meet the moving lips. She inhaled a quick pocket of air.

And then the world spun away from her as she climbed toward fulfillment.

And when it happened, she knew only the flaring sensation of beauty, of contentment and peace.

"Did I please you?" Julia said, her lips grazing lightly against Sue Ellen's shoulder.

"Oh yes, my darling. Yes." She sighed and drifted into a pasture of drowsiness. All the problems in her world were solved.

For once in her life, she did not have to make excuses or be afraid. She nestled against Julia's body and allowed sleep to take her.

A light nudging brought Sue Ellen awake. She smiled as Julia's lips touched hers.

"You're really a sleeper, aren't you?" Julia said.

She looked around and saw shadows beginning to slant out from the table and wooden chairs.

"Poor darling," Sue Ellen said. "Did I crush you?"

"I loved every moment of it." Her eyes were bright, the lids heavy and *lazy* over them.

Sue Ellen recollected herself. "I went to sleep without ..."

"Don't worry about that. Just tell me I made you happy."

"So happy." She put one palm on Julia's hip. "Really, are you sure we can't take care of you too?"

Julia shifted herself and sat up. "Frank will think we drowned or something." She lifted Sue Ellen up and made her get dressed.

CHAPTER EIGHT

"That afternoon was quite a revelation." Sue Ellen crossed her legs at the ankles and felt her silk stockings rub against each other.

"What exactly did you learn?" Dr. Ross pushed his chair back from the desk. The sound of the wooden legs against the nap of the rug pointed out his usual silence.

"Well, you know. I thought that boys and girls were made to fit. But I was so satisfied. But really satisfied. I didn't have to think about being pregnant. I didn't have to worry about anything at all. It kept popping into my mind that she must be a wizard to be able to do such a thing. And I was anxious to try it out on her."

"Would you say that it felt like a game?"

"That's exactly right. It was a funny game. I was almost ashamed that I hadn't thought it up myself. But there was another feeling too. Safety. The kind of safety that an infant must feel in its mother's arms. After all, Julia was the first woman who really came close to me, in every sense of the word. I wanted to be with her all the time. I wanted to hear her talk. Believe me, I was convinced that Julia was my salvation. If only Frank would go away."

"But you had the privacy of the beach house."

"Yes. I just didn't want to see Frank, though. He had made a fool of me. The first man in my life who had made me do something to him without satisfying me in return. I resented him. I hated him."

Frank was puttering with an old steam iron when Julia and Sue Ellen reached home. He had the parts spread out on the kitchen table and his fingernails were rimmed with grease.

Sue Ellen looked at him and saw a smudge of black across the bridge of his nose. She wished he woud go jump into a pot of boiling water.

"Long time no see," he said. A line of irritation deepened on either side of his mouth.

"Sue Ellen had a first dip in the balmy waters," Julia answered with fantastic casualness.

"Yeah, I notice."

The beginning of a sunburn flushed her cheeks. She surveyed Frank and considered yesterday's episode. He had gotten what he wanted. Why should he complain if she had gotten what she wanted?

At the same time Julia and Sue Ellen noticed an empty fifth of Scotch poking out from the aluminum garbage can. But Frank's hands were steady, his words precise.

"Why don't we have supper out?" Julia said.

Sue Ellen hoped that Frank would tell them to go by themselves. It would be lovely to have a private celebration with Julia.

"Sure, why not?" Frank said. "Maybe I'll meet some women who can like *me* for a change."

The words knifed Sue Ellen. She had taken for granted Frank's innocence about such matters as sex between two women. But apparently he knew all about his sister. And this thought led to another and more unpleasant one. If Frank knew, then there must have been many others for Julia. There might even be one right now. And yet Julia had been so concerned and so interested. The flicker of jealousy disappeared. After all, at seventeen she was not a virgin. Why should she expect this of Julia?

The three of them went to different parts of the house and changed for dinner.

In a grey suit Frank looked attractive again. He carried himself with an unconscious posture of erectness, as though he were marching. It appealed to Sue Ellen's weakness for virility. And she did not quite know how to cope with her contrasting emotions about Frank. On the one hand, she detested him. But as an object of masculinity, she enjoyed looking at him. Retreating from the problem, Sue Ellen concentrated her attention on Julia. A warmth of affection suffused her, recalling how the woman had done everything to please. The bottle green dress pegged slightly along the backs of her thighs, showing off a trimness every bit as delicious as Frank's masculinity. Sue Ellen walked between them, her arms linked in theirs.

They went to a sea food restaurant within walking distance. An orchestra played dance music softly in the background. Three couples moved on the polished floor while others sat chatting over cocktails. She would have liked to dance with Julia. The unfairness of life struck her hard, knowing that she could dance only with Frank.

She glanced over the menu, remembering the scattered stories she had heard about queers. One of the girls at school, a huge and bulky creature, gained the center of attention for two straight weeks by recounting her adventures in Greenwich Village. She had even gone so far as to bring snapshots of a girl friend dressed in trousers and a tie.

Julia could hardly be considered peculiar looking. Though she didn't have Sue Ellen's generous curves, her charms were none the less pleasing and none the less apparent. Oddly Sue Ellen did not think of herself as tainted in any way. Sex was in a compartment all by itself and not at all related to Sue Ellen Gaynor Hurley. She could go to bed with whomever she pleased. It gave her no names. The words pervert and normal had no meaning for her.

She allowed Frank to order a whiskey sour for her. By the time she had finished one, he had downed three Scotch and waters. Julia watched him but made no comment. She sat back with her elbow on the arm of the chair and watched the people dancing.

Was she thinking about Frank or was she perhaps recollecting the afternoon? Her unperturbed features displayed nothing but calm enjoyment of the atmosphere.

Between the drinks and the main course, Frank asked Sue Ellen to dance. She wanted to refuse. And yet Frank was feeling desolate again. His drunkenness showed itself by this aura of isolation. He looked steeped in loneliness, smothered, futile. Sue Ellen acquiesced and went with him to the dance floor.

He put his cheek against hers and she could easily watch Julia. The woman, self-composed, smiled back. Apparently she didn't mind that Frank held her so tightly. Or perhaps she was accustomed to his ways and had learned to tolerate them.

"I could make love to you tonight, Delilah." His voice was a whisper in her ear.

She felt his body lined against her own and it stirred her, but not for Frank. All Sue Ellen could think of was Julia's face when it was stripped of its composure.

"We could do things the way you like 'em," Frank said. "Nice soft bed. No mud, no bullets."

She let him talk. He couldn't insist right here on the dance floor. By the time they got home, Julia would take care of him. No doubt Julia knew how to attend to her brother. She wondered if they had ever fought over the same woman.

Frank insisted that they go home early. What he had in mind was very clear, but Julia pretended not to understand. She managed to convince him to go for a walk across the Causeway. The air would do him good.

And so they strolled and gazed out at Millionaire's Row, a strip of mansions, some lit, some dark, yachts resting quietly for the night at each private dock.

Despite Frank, Sue Ellen was enjoying the sights. Mink stoles worn on a night as warm as this amused her. And the passing thought entered her mind that perhaps Martin would enjoy vacationing here for awhile. She didn't want Julia to assume charge of her upkeep. Paying for the bathing suits was quite enough. She had three blank checks in her purse which Martin had signed and two hundred dollars in cash. By some standards she was a free agent. And yet... and yet.

To be alone with Julia. She wanted to know about the woman's life. From where she had gotten the strength to be so independent. No doubts, no fears, no anxieties seemed to assail her. She looked to be about thirty. Certainly not old for a woman. But what kind of life could she look forward to without family, without children? Had she been born content? Sue Ellen yearned to imitate her. She wanted to learn more of the secret which had only begun to unfold this afternoon.

Frank looked over into Biscayne Bay and its shimmering reflection of lights. "Wouldn't it be nice," he said down to the water, "if big sister went home and gave me a chance to make out with this lovely hunk of stuff waiting so patiently?"

Sue Ellen's lips came grimly together. Julia chuckled. "I think we'd better get us a cab," she said.

"No, I mean it," Frank turned and looked at her. "What perverse instinct always makes you hang around at the wrong times? There are plenty of women in this town. Enough for you. Enough for me. Why don't you give little brother a break for once? Home from the long wars and all that. How about it?"

"I guess I can make up my own mind," Sue Ellen said. The night wind blew her hair and separated it into whisps.

"You gonna choose heads or tails?" Frank laughed at his own humor.

If it weren't for Julia, she would have walked away and left him. But she had no desire to leave Julia. She felt a loyalty to the woman which was unexplainable in words.

Julia said, "We'll talk this over in the morning." A hint of impatience made her gesture briefly in the air.

These words were very strange to Sue Ellen. Was Julia consenting to a sharing policy? She looked at the woman sharply.

Julia winked. It was consolation but not consolation enough. She wanted Julia to be firm. Tell her brother where to get off.

"You know what I think?" Frank said. "I think that Lesbians should walk around with a great big L printed on their foreheads so guys like me wouldn't have to get stuck all the time. Live and let live, sure. But why do I always have to get fouled up by dikes? My own sister, no less."

"All right, Frank. That's enough." The firmness in Julia's voice pleased Sue Ellen. She moved a little closer to her.

"Yeah, I know," Frank muttered. "Always shut me up. The story of my life. Wish I was back in Deutchland. Someday I'm gonna tell you what it's like to really have a woman. I mean really. Like you could never know, butch sister."

His voice was too loud and strolling passersby turned to stare at the three of them. Julia was looking up and down the street for a cruising cab. One finally came along and she shoved Frank into it, with a feminine but efficient movement. They sped homeward and Frank settled into silence.

In the house Julia steered him off to his room, undressed him and got him under the covers. Sue Ellen listened to his various comments which floated all the way front to the living room where she sat, tensely smoking a cigarette. As an intruder in this household, she had no right to cause family trouble. She decided to leave in the morning. Find neutral quarters where she would be free to see Julia without interfering or hurting Frank. In a way she felt sorry for him. He recalled in her the memories of being ignored by her mother. Frank used Julia for a mother and she was betraying him now.

These confused thoughts spun and wove a fabric of uneasiness. When Julia came into her, she was all set to leave that very moment.

"I'm sorry about tonight," Julia said. She leaned over and cupped Sue Ellen's face in her hands. "It won't happen again. I'm going to see to it that Frank gets himself a job tomorrow."

"But that's not fair. I should leave. You know I should."

Julia bent over and kissed her. She let her hands slide down the girl's back. "Should you?" she whispered. "Do you really want to go?"

There was no answer. She wanted to leave and yet she could think of nothing more terrible than leaving her promise of happiness. "I think it would be best," her voice was uncertain. "Don't you?"

"I didn't think you were the kind of person to run away. And besides, it's much better for all concerned if we confine these goings on to our private domain. You understand. How would it look if I got you a room and kept coming up to see you? I'm a business woman, after all. Reputations are important. At least the figment of a reputation is."

Sue Ellen remembered the saleslady in the store. It didn't seem to her that Julia was really as discreet as she claimed. But the woman was too close to her for Sue Ellen to think clearly for very long. Her hand reached out and found Julia's breasts.

The doorbell rang.

They looked at each other for an instant. Julia went to answer. She returned with a yellow envelope.

"For you," she said. "Telegram."

Sue Ellen ripped open the flap and pulled out the folded paper.

"It's from Martin," she said. "He's coming down next Friday so we can spend the last week of my vacation together." She didn't know whether to be happy or sad. "It's crazy," she said.

"Well, isn't it nice to know he's so interested?"

"Of course." Her voice fell away with growing disappointment. "But I'd much rather spend my time with you."

"Oh, honey," Julia breathed. "You're so damned innocent. Despite everything."

Sue Ellen didn't understand. She looked at Julia questioningly and saw the lamplight pick out amusement in Julia's eyes.

"He's possessive, your Martin." She reached behind her and brought the table lighter up to the girl's second cigarette.

"Nonsense." Unconsciously the word imitated Julia's way of ridicule.

"All right, little girl. You'll see for yourself."

Julia took the cigarette away and crushed it out. Willingly Sue Ellen moved into the woman's arms. She reached under Julia's skirt to the warm, secret thighs. With her free hand, she pulled the lamp chain, thrusting their activities into darkness. But she wanted more room than the couch could give her. She slid down onto the floor and brought Julia with her.

"You're too much," Julia whispered. "I could make love to you from now till eternity."

Sue Ellen laughed low in her throat. She had already undone the front of the respectable green dress. "But not tonight," she murmured. "It's my turn to do the loving now."

A lusting greed to know everything before Martin's arrival consumed her. With perfect clarity, she remembered Julia's actions and proceeded to imitate them. Very soon, her natural instincts led Sue Ellen into by-paths of pleasure which Julia had not taught her.

The urge to aggression mounted within her. She wanted to possess Julia completely. A need to become one with the woman surged through her brain, befuddling all rational sense. A primitive memory, only half realized, tormented Sue Ellen. It was a memory of childhood and made Sue Ellen cry out, "Don't ever leave me. Promise you won't leave me!"

She hardly waited for an answer. Embracing Julia and holding on desperately, her torment mingled with passion.

The woman moaned beneath her touch. Her back arched in a taut curve of desire.

"Oh, yes …" Julia breathed. "Yes …"

Sue Ellen needed no urging. She gave to the woman with all the strength of her passion. She felt caught up in the whirlpool of sensation.

The woman trembled in her arms.

Then they lay quietly side by side. Seeing the release and the smile in Julia's eyes, she knew it had been fine. A great contentment filled her. She sighed as though a blessing had been bestowed.

Julia touched her chin with a forefinger. "You know," she murmured, "you have a real flair for this sort of thing."

Sue Ellen gazed up at the beams, dark in the roof. Julia's words were supposed to be a compliment, of course. And yet it felt like a left-handed kind of approval. There must be something else she was good for also. She wished Julia would tell her what it might be.

But this was hardly the time to discuss futures and careers. Sue Ellen rolled over into Julia's arms. The hunger in her own body was queerly unsated. It was a familiar feeling. These were the moments Sue Ellen dreaded facing, dreaded thinking about. A part of her had not been touched. An intangible compartment of her being remained apart. She could not define what she needed. Unable to cope with it, she forced it out of her mind. She pulled her legs up to her stomach and clasped her arms around her knees. Julia sat up and began straightening her clothes.

"Is something the matter, baby?"

"No. Of course not," Sue Ellen replied with all the affection she could muster.

"You look sad."

"Do I?" She made herself smile a little. If it were possible to explain to Julia, she would say it. Yet how could she speak of something so vague and elusive? Something which flitted in and out of her like a slippery shadow?

"I hope you trust me," Julia said. "You know I wouldn't hurt you for the world."

Yes, she knew. It had been only two days and still she felt closer to Julia than any other woman she had ever known. Restlessly she turned over onto her side and stared at the leg of a chair. Now was the time to grasp what was bothering her and say it out. Julia would help. If anyone could help her, certainly Julia was the person. But the feeling refused to crystalize. She fought to catch it and make it plain. Nothing happened. The emotion sped away into darkness.

"Maybe it's Frank," she said.

"I don't think so." Julia reached up to the table and brought down two cigarettes. "Bad conscience, perhaps?"

"About what?" Sue Ellen inquired with all innocence.

"Maybe I'm too sensitive," Julia said. "Let's just forget it, shall we?"

Sue Ellen inhaled smoke deep into her lungs. Better forgotten indeed. She was being childish. Maybe acting like a spoiled brat. Her gaze fastened on Julia's fingers steadily holding the crisp cigarette. How she envied Julia's knowledge of herself. The woman knew her limitations and how to use her assets. In contrast Sue Ellen realized how little she really knew about her own person. She felt like a watery substance which took the shape of any vessel that held it.

Her mind reached out for something familiar. Martin would soon be here.

CHAPTER NINE

"That was a terrible moment."

Dr. Ross waited silently as she grasped for words to describe the feeling.

"I was a big girl, actually. And I felt so very little. You might say I felt as though I hadn't been born yet. Incomplete. Waiting. Waiting for what, I didn't know. I still don't."

For the first time Sue Ellen realized that she was beginning to tie her past to the here and now. All the episodes with her father in Virginia, with Jeff and Martin, with her mother ... these things had lived in a special file, opened now and again for inspection. But now as she recalled Julia, she felt that it was something which influenced her still. Her throat tightened.

"I think I'm scared," she said. She waited now, hoping Dr. Ross would say something to comfort her. "I'm really very frightened. It feels like someone has left me on a desert island and sailed away. Maybe I'm going to die. But that's childish. I'm here in this office. You're here. When the hour is up, I'll go out the door."

But the feeling persisted. A tiny pulse beat started in her jaw and tapped its way down the length of her neck. She gasped for air. The room felt stale.

"Will you please open the window?"

"There's plenty of ventilation. It never bothered you before."

"Of course. I'm silly."

"What's frightening you? What are you thinking of?"

"I don't know," she replied truthfully. "My mind is an absolute blank and yet .... I'm thinking of the bones on my mother's chest. You know how a chicken looks when the meat is eaten off it? My mother looked like that when I went to visit her in the hospital. I loved Julia. I really loved her desperately."

"Did you?"

"Yes. Yes. She wanted to help me. It wasn't my fault. I couldn't communicate or she would have helped me. I wanted to tell her how much I loved her. The words wouldn't come."

"Did you ever tell your mother that you loved her?"

It was a horrible question. She wanted to whirl around and hit Dr. Ross. "But she hated me. She didn't want to hear if I loved her or not. She hurt Daddy. She left him. She called him all sorts of names that weren't true." Her voice was very loud now and high pitched. "I didn't love her. I hated her all the time. Why should I have loved her?"

"But you needed her," Dr. Ross persisted. "When you were very young, someone had to feed you, take care of you."

"Not her. She couldn't do that. It was beneath her, messing around with babies. Clellie took care of me."

"Do you remember?"

"No, but I know it in my heart. Mother didn't want to look at me. I think she hated me even before I was born. Spoiled her figure."

"When did she say that?"

"I took it for granted."

"Why?"

"I don't know. ... I don't know ...." Sue Ellen's wall of reserve crumbled and slid away. Burning choking sobs consumed her. She put her fist into her mouth, trying to stifle the sound.

"You see," Dr. Ross said, "there comes a point in analysis when some of the little things which have been locked in the closet of the subconscious rise to the surface and must be dealt with. It's a difficult, drawn out affair. One makes three steps forward and two back. But gradually all the feelings we have been trying to evade become feelings which fit into a pattern and must be recognized. As you pour out thousands of words, I try to find the recurring ideas which make your particular pattern. And then you must see them for yourself. Realization and more realization until gradually we weaken and break these destructive patterns. Slowly you replace them with healthier ones. I think that one might consider psychology to be the science of common sense."

Sue Ellen had found a handkerchief in her purse and dried her lashes. "Yes, I know," she said in a voice which still trembled. "I might hate my mother, but I didn't want to. I wanted her to love me so I could love her back. Maybe I knew it all the time it was happening. But how can you want for your mother to love you, when that's what a mother is supposed to do without being asked? Martin loved me." She realized there was no logical connection between the two. But just the sound of Martin's name on her lips was a source of refuge.

In the few days before Martin was due to come down to Florida, Sue Ellen vacillated between eagerness and antagonism. Martin would get a place to stay at one of the nicer hotels and, of course, she would stay with him. This would relieve her of the responsibility of herself. He would think for her, escort her, protect her. She wouldn't have to face Frank every day. Her role in Martin's life was very comfortable. She could handle him almost without thinking. The security he gave her was worth every sacrifice.

And then she would think, was it worth the sacrifice of Julia? She had never learned to be sneaky and it did not occur to her that it was possible to keep both relationships going, undiscovered. Julia was important in a way very different from her stepfather. She promised Sue Ellen a new understanding of life. Of herself. Through Julia she hoped to discover her own identity. With her step-father, she was the coquettish little girl. With Julia she felt the first grapplings with adulthood. Both were precious. Both seemed vitally necessary.

She went with Julia to the shop propelled by a vague desire to see just how people go about earning their own living. The ways of business were a mystery to her and she had never been interested in unravelling them. From her mother she had unconsciously absorbed the attitude that it as the man's responsibility to do the providing. A woman need only know how to spend. She need only have sufficient intelligence, or cunning, to provide herself with a man who had the wherewithal to spend. Money, for Sue Ellen, had become a just reward for being female.

But Julia's very existence proved that there were other, more satisfying approaches to living. And she was glad to take Sue Ellen to the shop. Sue Ellen's appearance provided a good model for the jewelry. The structure of her face carried dangling earrings and clips with equal grace. The ample expanse of her bosom made a more complimentary backdrop for necklaces than the velvet show pads. She might not know the techniques of selling, but her appearance was its own salestalk.

Besides, both Sue Ellen and Julia knew that it was better for the girl to be in the store all day than for her to wander alone in a strange town.

Talking with a variety of women, most of whom were at leisure and pleased with themselves, was a gratifying experience. Gradually Sue Ellen found herself suggesting different ensembles or more complimentary styling for the various shapes and demeanors. She spoke to these women, not as a salesgirl, but as a friend. Her instinctive good taste and natural approach resulted in the writing of more sales-slips.

When she asked Julia how she was doing, the resultant smile and nod was more of an encouragement than any words.

For four days Sue Ellen had a grand time. And her nights were filled with a sharing which gave peace to the racing emotions demanding their claim to attention. It was not, by any means, a child's unquestioning contentment. But the inside hungers were sated enough so that they did not scream in craving.

When the time came for Sue Ellen to meet Martin's plane, she felt as though she were actually deserting the store. The week had engulfed her in a way of life demanding attention away from herself. Its various complexities showed her a new world and she had become a willing part.

Riding in the cab to the airport, she kept revising how she would tell Martin about her new experience. Would he approve? Would he think this work beneath her? And she wondered to explain about Julia without dwelling too tenderly.

She stood in the waiting room and listened to the loudspeaker blaring its announcement of departures and arrivals. Eager, tanned people clasping strangely pale newcomers amused and pleased her. She had only a slight pinkness. There had been no time for sun bathing. It was a proud sensation to know her time had been spent more profitably than lolling on the sand.

"Susie!"

She saw Martin shoulder through the crowd as he always did, unconsciously using his mountainous bulk to make a special path.

Their arms went around each other. She smelled the homey odor of his worsted suit. Visions of being a businesswoman vanished. Once again, she became the Persian kitten.

"Miss me?" he said, taking her with him to the baggage counter. "The apartment's been haunted without you."

"Yes, it has been strange," she breathed, "alone."

But her mind was not on their conversation so much as on the contemplation of his appearance. As though for the first time, she saw the silver grey of his hair. It shocked her to realize that Martin wasn't a young man. She had always considered him ageless, when she considered his age at all. Now she was suddenly sure that Martin was much older than she realized. The wrinkles around the edges of his eyes were not laugh lines. They were worry lines, age lines. The heaviness of his jaw a sign of lessening body activity. She felt annoyingly distressed to see Martin with such objectivity. Even the little curls of hair which came out from beneath the jacket sleeve had sprinkles of grey in them. It dawned on Sue Ellen that he was actually and truly old enough to be her father.

"Come on," he said, lifting the valise as though it were empty. "We're going to live it up before you have to go back to school. Know something? It's been snowing in New York."

She went with Martin to the convertible Chevvy he had rented for his stay, not caring very much about the snow, hoping that he would say something that had more of an adult ring to it.

They moved away from the airport almost before Sue Ellen had the door closed. Martin drove with a heavy foot on the gas pedal. His thick shoulders and arms seemed to have more horsepower than the engine. She wondered why they had to race so. Perversely her mind kept repeating that Martin's days were numbered.

"I really am glad to be away from all that silence night after night."

He had already said this. "What about Jeff?" she asked aimlessly.

"Jeff? That boy's dead and doesn't know how to lie down beneath a tombstone. Never saw a young boy stare into so many textbooks. You'd think he didn't study all winter long at school. Great pal, Jeff."

"Well, law is a complicated thing." The clock on the dashboard said three. Julia would be taking a coffee break in the little back room. She drank much too much coffee.

Martin squeeled the car around a corner. "I guess we have more interesting things to talk about than the young barrister. Been living it up all by yourself?"

"Not really." Sue Ellen had never felt less alone in her life than during the past week with Julia.

"You don't look like you've been conquering the ocean."

Sue Ellen couldn't understand why he was talking about everything that didn't matter. She remembered all the good times they used to have together. And she wanted it to be like that now.

"You'll never guess what I've been doing," she said, in an effort to make their conversation more important.

"Boozing?" He laughed and touched her affectionately on the knee.

"Don't be silly."

They were driving past the rows of luxurious hotels. Martin's attention diverted to finding the one where they would be staying. He wasn't in a mood to be serious. Perhaps anything she might say wouldn't be important enough to get beyond his holiday mood.

"I've been working," she announced.

"Not you too?" An eyebrow went up in disappointment.

"I didn't say studying. Working. A real job."

They slowed for a red light and now Martin examined her with interest. "I don't understand." He took a cigar from his inside jacket pocket and clamped it unlit between his teeth.

"Supposing I tell you all about it when we're upstairs?" she said. Having caught his attention, she felt placated. It was about time that Martin began to realize that she was more than a beloved toy.

He questioned her for the few short blocks to their hotel but she stubbornly resisted giving him any further information.

The doorman took the keys to the car and a bell boy came out for Martin's suitcase. They entered a fabulous lobby decorated with mosaic walls and violet draperies. Martin seemed preoccupied with Sue Ellen's announcement as he signed the register. He hardly heard the manager's spiel. Ashamed of the little smirk tilting up the corners of her mouth, Sue Ellen felt pleased, nevertheless, that she had finally made a dent in him.

They rode up in the elevator quietly. Sue Ellen patted her hair nonchalantly and tilted her head in an impersonal but pleasant greeting to another male passenger.

When they got inside Martin barely took time enough to tip the porter and toss the keys on the bed before turning to Sue Ellen.

"Now, what was all that you were saying?" He was even too interested to kiss her.

She went to the mirror and loosened one of the earrings she had forgotten to return to Julia. "You make it sound like a catastrophe."

"Make *what* sound like a catastrophe?" He took the cigar and jammed it into his handkerchief pocket.

"An honest day's work never hurt anybody."

"Will you kindly stop this double talk?" His nostrils flared slightly. She saw the tendons in his neck tighten.

For an instant she felt a wave of regret. She hadn't intended to worry Martin. Her little game was giving the whole thing too much importance. As a result, he might get angry with Julia. That would be too embarrassing. Julia treated her like an adult. She couldn't let Martin spoil that impression.

"Really, it's nothing at all." She came over and loosened his tie. "I met a boy on the train. Since I didn't have a hotel reservation … but I told you all that. Well, his sister. You see, she has this jewelry store. I thought it would be fun to do something instead of loaf. Anyway, I knew you were coming down. For a few days, what difference could it make?" She kissed him on the chin and took his hands in her own. "Why don't we just forget it now that we're together? I really did miss you, you know."

She could tell that he wanted to pursue the subject further. To prevent it, she stood up on her toes and kissed him on the mouth. He tried to draw away. Sensing the backward movement of his head before the actual motion, she reached up along the bristles of his neck and held him steady, continuing to move her lips across his. With one hand she managed to unbutton his jacket, then pressed herself against the thin material of his shirt. She knew his weakness for the lushness of her body. And as they touched, she felt a growing desire within herself. There was something about the touch of another human being... something that tantalized and goaded. A sense of the forbidden aroused a perverse desire to own and be possessed in return.

Even before she knew that Martin was responding, she was undressing him. All recollection of Julia faded. The job no longer existed. She didn't care where she was. Or with whom. Yes, Martin loved her. Yet beyond this was something more vital. Warm, living flesh. Together with someone behind a secure wall of need. For this moment, nothing could come between them. All threats of insecurity disappeared. And, above all, she herself was important. More important than anybody for the person who wanted her as she wanted.

They fell together onto the bed. She held Martin trapped in the web of passion. She wanted only to seek and find oblivion in the arms of this man who loved her. She ran her tongue across his lips. Her fingertips caressed the muscles of his chest.

He was quick to respond. From long habit he knew just how to fondle her.

"Oh, Susie, I've missed you," his lips spoke against her throat.

She could feel the warm vapor of his words on her flesh.

"I need you," she murmured, as though it had been a million years since the last time.

Her back arched, her full hips rose eagerly, envisioning and sensing the moment of contact before it happened. She gasped on an intake of breath.

And it was even better than she had remembered it. All the problems, the troubles she had known vanished from her consciousness and they drifted together in a chasm of forgetfulness.

Sue Ellen tilted her head back against the pillow and sighed with contentment.

Martin patted her forehead with the edge of the sheet. "I really did miss you," he said almost to himself.

Now that it was over she knew that the problem would return, undiminished. With an odd feeling of having accomplished nothing at all, Sue Ellen realized that she still had to explain about Julia. What had made her think that the union of their bodies would change anything? She stared up at the corners of the ceiling and listened to the oiled purring of the air conditioner. But he'll be more congenial now, she thought. It wasn't true, though, and she knew it. Martin was far from stupid. Her body could not blind him. Why, then, had she deluded herself? The joke, of course, was on her. And she was not surprised. But she felt distinctly uncomfortable. The sneaking suspicion intruded itself that she had used Martin simply as an excuse for sex. But she could have him anytime without an excuse.

That vague discomfort which she felt the first night with Julia fled through her again. She closed her eyes and nestled against Martin, hoping that sleep would rescue her. She didn't want to talk to him about anything.

Restlessly she waited for drowsiness. Encircled by huge arms, she should feel safe and take for granted her place in the world. The elusive feeling stubbornly refused to arrive. At last she pulled away from him.

"I guess I can't sleep in the middle of the day," she said. "I'll take a shower and we'll go out for something to eat. Poor dear, you must be starved. And here I was, being so inconsiderate."

"Don't chastize yourself too strenuously," he grinned.

As she powdered and dressed after her bath, Sue Ellen waited for him to suggest that she take him to meet her new friends. If she knew Martin, he would want to treat them to dinner. He would want to satisfy himself about the kind of persons she had chosen to be with in his absence.

Expectantly she waited this suggestion as Martin, in turn, showered and put on a fresh tan suit. The idea of showing Julia off a little was actually gratifying, despite the dangers involved. Julia. Someone to be proud of. Very different from high school kids. After meeting her new friend, Martin would begin to see that she was growing up.

She waited and waited but Martin said nothing. He took her downstairs to the dining room. The *maitre de* led them to a table for two and Martin ordered for both, confident that he knew Sue Ellen's taste. She watched him squeeze lemon juice onto a segment of papaya. He looked as if there were nothing more important in the world than sharing a wonderful dinner with her.

The dining room began to crowd with people and the clatter of dishes taken off and returned to heavy metal trays. She noticed other women observing her and Martin, probably conjecturing about the relationship between them. And Martin saw nothing, concerned himself with nothing beyond the ham steak, the wine and finally, a brandy with ginger ale.

The food in her belly did not make Sue Ellen any more content. She chafed for Martin's curiosity to return. When he finally led her out onto the back porch, Sue Ellen could stand it no longer. She let him walk with her for a short distance beside the empty pool. They reached the railing which overlooked a serene ocean glowing with the last orange reflections of the sun. She put her arm through his and said, "Julia's very anxious to meet you, after all I've told her."

She didn't dare look at him. But she felt a slight movement of his elbow.

"And what did you tell her?" he asked, with a nonchalance that didn't sound quite sincere.

"Oh, everything," she replied innocently, her gaze still resting on the horizon.

"Everything?"

Sue Ellen felt herself smile inside. Now she had done it. Martin certainly would not let the matter drop without investigating precisely what she meant by everything.

CHAPTER TEN

"I wanted attention. I wanted Martin to be really concerned. I wanted Julia to see that she had plenty of competition. Not consciously. Only now, as I think back on it, does it begin to make any sense." Sue Ellen paused in an effort to search out motives.

Dr. Ross cleared his throat and recrossed his legs. She didn't have to look at him to know the little movements he made. The sense of sound was a language all its own that she was beginning to know unconsciously.

"You'd think that a bright kid would know when to leave well enough alone. I don't think I was stupid. Maybe I was purposely looking for trouble."

"Trouble?" Dr. Ross's voice indicated that he wanted her to explain further.

"Trouble. Excitement. The limelight. Anything you want to call it. Anyway, I wanted them to fight over me. I was infatuated with Julia and I wanted to convince myself that I could trust her."

"Did you trust Martin?"

"You know something, doctor. I don't think I ever trusted anybody in my whole life. Not completely. When my father didn't answer my letters, I lost faith in him. Mother, we don't even have to speak about." She felt the bitterness surge for a moment. "Jeff. He was interested in only one thing and when that stopped, so did our friendship. And poor Martin. I knew I was using him. It was very unsatisfying. If just once he would have been strict with me, maybe things would have turned out differently." Sue Ellen sighed. A profound sense of loneliness invaded her. "And Julia. Well, I couldn't let myself go with her. It was just a week we had together anyway. It didn't occur to me that she had any reason to return my interest in full measure. There had been others for her. I didn't feel special in her life. But God knows I wanted to. And so I had to pit her against Martin. I wanted her to fight and win me away from him. Then I would have been satisfied that she really cared. But at the time I didn't understand these things. All I knew was this driving compulsion to bring them together."

Sue Ellen knew that one of Martin's weak points was his sense of dignity. He never talked about her mother in the hospital. He never considered the possibility of getting a divorce. If he thought that she had divulged their private life to a stranger, he would have to investigate to see how much of their reputation Sue Ellen had destroyed.

"Maybe it would be nice if I thanked your friend properly for taking care of you this past week," Martin said, turning his back on the water and glaring around at the crystals of sand scattered beside the pool.

"Yes, I think so," she answered brightly. He wasn't being difficult at all. Martin responded as she knew he must. His habit of giving her everything she wanted made him very agreeable to live with.

"Supposing I phone and see if she's home now," she said.

Automatically Martin reached in his pocket for a dime.

When she returned to him, Sue Ellen felt like a woman of accomplishment.

"Julia will be over in an hour," she announced.

She saw his large hands gripping the rail and wondered why the metal didn't squash between his fingers. "The least you could have done was offer for us to pick her up," he said coldly. The usual sparkle in his eyes was a masculine glitter now. This was probably how he looked at a business meeting.

Sue Ellen felt a moment of uneasiness. She wasn't accustomed to this sharp determination. But, of course, it would have been stupid to invite themselves into Julia's home. Frank might be there. Or he could come in at any time. She had to avoid him completely. Loud mouth. Drunk. Why had she allowed him to touch her?

"You've had enough riding for one day," she murmured. "After all, it is your vacation."

A disgruntled sound came from him. But he was quieting.

"Let's go inside and dance until she comes. I just love any excuse to be close to you."

She had never manipulated Martin quite so consciously. A touch of shame mingled with her excitement.

"You're a funny girl," Martin said, following her beside the beach chairs.

A sun dried odor emanated from the canvas chairs. How many bodies they had held. She wanted to sit down in one and absorb its memories of naked, languid flesh. The crinoline stuff which held her skirt in a flare felt stiff and prudish by contrast. The decorum of her appearance restrained Sue Ellen from the wanton gesture of flinging herself into a chair. She knew she looked well groomed and lovely. Glances in the dining room, glances in the lobby had told her so. Not many women could wear scarlet. They would be lost in its vitality. Sue Ellen had no such fear. Privately she laughed at women who were afraid to wear clothes that emphasized breasts and hips. She enjoyed letting the world see her good body. After all, bodies made love. And love was more important than anything. Wars were fought because of love. Cleopatra had brains. So did Madame Pompadour. A king's courtesan got more attention than his wife. Every woman knew that. But few of them had the courage to take advantage of this understanding.

They entered the hotel's night club and Sue Ellen approved of all the men who looked at her. She ordered a plain Seven-Up, so that she would be in command of herself when Julia arrived. Confident of the situation, she let her mind dwell on the various men seated at the bar. She felt happy enough with Martin, but the range of possibilities intrigued her. She had heard that each man did it differently. There could be interesting surprises in store for her. To be tied to one man felt very unfair. Especially an old man. It wasn't her fault that Martin had lived his life through already. Hers was just beginning. The appreciative glances beckoned to her. She wanted to go over and talk to some of the younger men. Their mouths promised sensation. Their interest promised attention. It was grand to be attractive. It was unfair to be chained to Martin.

She heard a snap and saw that Martin had broken the plastic stirring rod in two.

"Your mind is way off someplace, isn't it?" he said.

"No, not at all," she protested. "I've never been in a place like this. I'm just looking around to see what I can see."

"And what do you see?"

She shrugged. The gold heart on its gold chain slid down into her cleavage. "People, I guess. What else is there?"

A long breath escaped from between his lips. "I guess it was bound to happen." The note of sadness returned her attention to him completely.

Martin wasn't a fool. Nor was it fair for her to lie. Still, she didn't want to lose him. What was more disastrous than a woman alone, unprotected?

"You're overworked," she replied. "Let's do that cha-cha you learned and forget the world."

She got him out onto the dance floor, knowing that the men at the bar were curious to see her move that generous body around. She loved the feeling of dance. It gave one permission to shake and wiggle and twist and still appear to be a lady. Martin was an adequate dancer. He didn't detract from her in any way. So long as he kept in rhythm, she was free to thrust herself about, give leeway to the nervous pressures demanding that she move. Her breasts jiggled voluptuously. The sensation aroused her. She felt the flesh of her thighs twitching delightfully as the silk stockings rubbed against each other. Her hair swung from one shoulder to the other. She felt gratified to see men turning their backs to the bar so that they could observe her unobstructed. The bongo rhythm urged and goaded. Pungency of liquor, mixing with the smokey air, teased her. Her feet were confident on the waxed floor. She grinned widely, tilting back her head.

And then, standing at the entrance, was Julia. Julia watching her. Sue Ellen caught Martin's hand, stopped the movement of her body and tried to breath normally.

Julia remained at the door, serene in a sheath dress that hugged her in satin blackness. One could see nothing, yet one could see everything of the uptilted breasts and sleek rib cage merging into the compact hips.

Sue Ellen led Martin to her. She introduced them and watched Julia extend one gloved hand in greeting. Onyx and silver earrings swung in a note of sleek casualness. Julia, complete, preserved, sure.

The three of them returned to the table. Sue Ellen wanted to splash her face with cold water and dry away the film of perspiration which had gathered along her hairline.

Julia ordered a Scotch sour and all of them waited for someone to begin conversation. Their eyes touched and fled, each guarding his own knowledge.

Sue Ellen blurted, "Isn't she beautiful?" then cursed herself for the obvious indiscretion.

"Indeed," Martin said thoughtfully, raising his own glass in tribute.

But anyone could have said this about Julia. Her evening make-up sculptured the almond tilt of her eyes. The total effect of her features was a soft precision demanding respect. She took the compliment with a slight nod, retaining her poise.

Martin said, "I thank you for looking after my daughter. I trust she hasn't been too much trouble."

"To the contrary." Julia's lips pursed on the rim of her glass. She lowered the drink to the table and extracted a cigarette from a thin case. "Sue Ellen had been very helpful."

Her voice was casual enough. No hint of hidden meanings, no private smirk. It occurred to Sue Ellen that both these people had reputations to care for. Only she herself had nothing to lose as a result of this meeting. Would there be no fireworks, then? Would each pretend ignorance about the other for the sake of reputations? She sighed with a tremor of irritation.

"I was hoping to talk Martin into letting me stay on with you for a while." She took her own cigarette, wishing that Julia would light it for her unconsciously.

Martin brought the flame quickly upward for her. It felt like an act of possession. She recalled Julia's words, about the reason Martin had come down to Florida. Yet if Martin were feeling unsure of her, he certainly wasn't showing it.

The band had shifted to a tango rhythm. It gave the room a feeling of intimacy, weaving a common thread of promise among all the strangers. She gazed beyond the point of flame to one of the young men at the bar. He stared hard, trying to discover if Sue Ellen would accept his offer of a dance, she thought. She let a smile flicker just for him in her eyes.

"I never considered you the working type," Martin said and it took her a moment to remember the trend of their conversation.

"I'm changing every day," she answered and her gaze shifted to Julia. But Julia's answering nod had all the camouflage of ordinary acquaintanceship. She seemed far away, as though they had never touched in lingering desire.

"Well, that's up to you of course." Martin drained his glass and motioned for the waiter.

Why doesn't she say something that'll make his eyes pop? A flush of hatred fired through her. Cowards. Purposefully she gazed back to the fellow at the bar and licked her lips with a subtle movement. For her there was no implication in the gesture beyond a wish to get even with these people who really didn't care for her at all. When it came to a showdown, here they were, both ducked deep into their shells, hoping the threatening enemy would go away without a fight.

The man mashed out his cigarette and started for their table. In the shadows she could not tell the actual color of his hair. But as he came closer, she saw the highlights of auburn. His features had a tone of prettiness about them. No doubt he liked to admire himself in the mirror. It was a special compliment to Sue Ellen that so obviously choosy a person found her worthy.

He cleared his throat and placed three finger tips on the tablecloth. "Pardon me."

Sue Ellen hardly waited for him to verbalize his request for this dance before starting to move herself out from behind the table.

Martin said, "Yes. Of course," in an amused though startled voice.

I'll fix them both good, she thought, drifting into the stranger's arms.

She moved herself closer to him than the touch of his palm beneath her shoulderblades required.

His after shave lotion exuded a flowery odor that went with the meticulous appearance. And he danced smoothly, sure of the steps and of his control over her yielding body.

"You are a most appealing young woman," he said. The words were formally strung together as though he had learned English from a textbook. His hint of accent held a glamorous appeal for Sue Ellen. It lent an incongruous virility to him.

"You are a most appealing young man." She wanted to flirt with him so that the others would see and be jealous. Not one glance did she intend to waste on anything but him. Let them suffer. Let them doubt.

As though the orchestra were on her side of the game, it cooperated by playing a long medley. They didn't need to talk very much. His hands spoke with their touch on her waist. The pressure of his fingers was like kisses along her back. A flaring torch of interest seered through her. Martin might not care, Julia might not care. But this stranger was interested. He would like to possess her. No doubt he could even love her if she gave him the chance. Their closeness fogged her brain. Her thoughts raced down familiar channels, leading to an exotic bedroom. She felt his lips against her ear and the soft breath from his nostrils. It did not matter where he came from or who he was. This moment, this reality of having another person desiring her, was all that she needed.

"I would like to go with you," Sue Ellen whispered.

"That would be most enchanting," he whispered in return. "My room number. It is six-eleven. I will wait."

When the dance ended he brought her ceremoniously back to the table, bowed and retired to the bar.

"That was lovely," she sighed and leaned back against the wall, pretending that she was speaking to herself.

"I didn't think he was quite your speed," Martin said. She heard a strange tightness in his voice. It disturbed the throbbing in her own heart. Shaken back to the situation, she looked at him. His naturally ruddy complexion was drained. For an instant she wanted to apologize. But the throbbing returned in a greater surging violence. Her mind refused to leave the image she had of herself and the stranger naked in each other's arms. That insistent feeling made her hurt. It struggled almost beyond her control. She picked up Julia's glass and drained its contents.

"We've been talking about you," Julia said as though it weren't quite apparent. "Martin has agreed that if you want to spend the rest of your vacation working, you may do so."

"Oh?"

"You have a wise father. Be grateful for him."

"I am." But she couldn't concentrate on the job or on being grateful for Martin. A madness possessed her. The flowery odor had remained in her nostrils, dragging her by some magic to look for the stranger.

When she glanced at the bar, he had gone.

"Maybe you need to get your feet on the ground," Martin offered. He put his hand over hers.

His hand felt chill and Sue Ellen had to restrain herself from drawing her own away.

"Nine thirty tomorrow morning," Julia said.

"Yes. Fine." She recollected herself. "Thank you, Martin. It'll be good for me. You'll see."

"I hope so."

Six hundred eleven. He must be getting undressed now. A maroon robe of silk. Brandy snifter perhaps. No. Naked. Lying on the bed. Stroking the pillow case and making believe it's my breast.

She had to get away. The need to be with the stranger was making her nauseous with its wild, unfulfillable need.

"Will you excuse me?" she said. "I have to …"

The sentence unfinished, she got up and left the room. No concern about what they might think impeded her. Forcing herself not to run, she got to the elevator. It rose to the sixth floor and she hurried along the corridor. Footsteps inside came closer.

"This is good fortune," he said as she barged in. "I did not expect you so soon."

Still completely dressed, he held a silver hair brush in one hand.

"Hurry," she said, tugging at the belt of her dress.

"Oh, it is a shame to hurry such a beautiful evening."

Sue Ellen hardly heard him. And if she did, it would not have mattered. Without looking where they landed, she flung her clothes away. One image, and one image only, demanded completion. His fingers did not move fast enough with the buttons of his own clothes. She reached over and helped.

Her body did not need to be awakened further. He kissed her and she needed more than kisses. A chair was closer than the bed. She made him sit on it and flung herself onto his lap.

The movements of her own body were sufficient for them both. She pounded herself against him in the violence of her need. And in just a few moments her chin collapsed against his shoulder.

"You Americans," he said. "When will you ever learn?"

"I'll be back," she said. "And there'll be lots more." But even to her own ears, the words were empty. Now that it was over, she knew she did not care about him. He could have a thousand faces, a thousand personalities and it would be the same. Only one thing counted. And she had used him well for her purpose.

In the small bathroom, she doused her face with water and reapplied make-up. Then she slid back into her underthings, adjusted the dress, ran a comb through her hair and left him.

Riding back down in the elevator, she could hardly believe what had happened. Her senses once again intact, she tried to reconstruct the reasons which had led her to a strange man's room. Not even to know his name! A cold wave of fear began to consume her. Was she mad? Who ever heard of doing such a thing? Why, she might even be pregnant. A wave of remorse made her want to cry in Julia's arms. Julia, who wanted her, cared enough to put up such an elaborate front for Martin. Julia, whom she had betrayed for no reason. She clutched her purse, trying to steady herself. Her mind flipped back to that terrible night when she thought it was a radio program coming from her mother's room. And she was like her mother. So much like her mother. Her teeth came together hard and she closed her eyes.

A promise, she thought. I promise, on my life, never ever to do such a thing again. I will control myself if I have to burst.

The idea of sex became suddenly repulsive. She would have no trouble with it in the future. All she would have to do is remember her mother and she felt confident that the desire would fade.

When she came out of the elevator, she took a deep breath and strolled very erect into the right club.

"Are you all right?" Martin asked. He stood up as she sat down. "Can I get you something?"

"No. I'm fine. Please don't bother." Through a mist of tenderness, she gazed at Julia. Never would she tell her what had taken place. She would spare Julia the pollution.

"Perhaps you should get to bed early," Julia said. "It's going to be a hard day tomorrow. Saturday always is."

Sue Ellen felt the woman examining her with a hidden understanding that made her wish she were invisible.

"You're right," Sue Ellen said. "I could use a good night's sleep."

They both relaxed, apparently glad that Sue Ellen had agreed to an early end for the evening.

Martin called for the check. "Why don't you run along upstairs and I'll drive Julia home."

"All right," she said, glad for the opportunity to be alone with herself. Silently she thanked Julia for understanding this need.

Sue Ellen went up to the room and got undressed. Her legs trembled and a feverish warmth suffused her. Martin had, of course, taken a separate room for her and she locked the door, praying that he wouldn't want to come in. She felt as though a hand had tightened on her brain, squeezing the sense out of it. Her mind refused to go back and examine what had happened. She climbed into the bed and hugged a pillow tightly to her in a mute agony. The experience of sex did not bother her. But how could she have been driven by so animal a compulsion? Despairingly she cried out for some protection, some assurance that what had occurred was only a freak. It must never happen again. It must not dare.

A placid breeze sighed at the curtains as she tried to believe in herself and in her ability to prevent this again. The more she thought, the more uncertain she became. A torment embraced her in hungry arms and burning tears swelled her eyelids. Unknown to herself, her lips murmured, "Daddy ... Daddy."

She heard the door knob rattle. An hour must have passed. Maybe two or three.

"Who is it?"

"It's me, Martin. Are you sure you're all right?"

"Yes. Yes. Go to sleep."

"I'd like a word with you."

"Can't it wait?"

"Just a word." His voice pleaded. She sat up. The room was dark. Clouds riding across the high moon would keep her swollen eyelids in shadow. She padded barefoot to the door and opened it.

"Please don't put on the light," she said. "I have a headache."

"You scared me," he said, coming inside and sitting down on the backless chair of her dressing table.

Sue Ellen went back and sat down on the edge of the bed. "Maybe I had too much sun today."

"Anyhow, I wanted to tell you that it's all right if you want to work for Julia. At first I thought ... Well, older women preying on young girls. You know. A person can't be too careful. But she's not one of those."

His voice had a ridiculous conviction that made Sue Ellen forget her trouble.

"How could you think such a stupid thing," she said, glad that the light was out so he couldn't see her struggle not to laugh.

"Experience. But experience is a pretty narrow-minded way of judging people, isn't it?"

"I'm glad you're convinced."

"I just wanted you to know."

"Thank you." She got back between the covers and pulled them up over her shoulders. "Now I'd really better get to sleep. Will you wake me in the morning?"

"Sure thing." He came over and kissed her on the forehead. "You're a wiser girl than I knew, little Susie. Maybe work will give you something that I couldn't. And when you graduate, we'll see about finding you a job if you still want one. Good night, angel."

She waited until he had closed the door and then gave vent to silent but raucous laughter.

It was a strange feeling. She had never before laughed about something that didn't strike her funny.

All at once, she couldn't stand the thought of Martin in her life. Martin, her protector, duped in fifteen minutes flat. Her world became a slippery globe with no handles for her to hang onto. She felt herself sliding off and falling, falling into space. No one could really take care of her.

The only way out was to take care of herself. She must learn everything Julia knew and more. How to fool men. How to fool women. Love was a figment of the imagination. It was a straw doll which, handled too roughly, tore and drained all its meaning into a little heap of nothingness. All that existed was oneself. Alone. Starved. Ignored.

How could she trick herself into believing that there was such a thing as unselfishness? It was Sue Ellen for Sue Ellen. And everyone else be damned.

CHAPTER ELEVEN

Dr. Ross had a way of looking at her which made Sue Ellen feel that there were lots of people yet to be discovered who weren't afraid to share themselves with strangers. She told this to him.

"One could put it that way," Dr. Ross said. "I might add that when a person knows who he is, and what he is capable of, it becomes easier to be oneself with strangers and friends alike. I don't think it is possible for any person to be totally uninhibited. But we hope that the process of psychoanalysis helps one to trim away the needless inhibitions imposed by environment. The memory of a past fear can bring on a smaller fear in a present situation where the emotion is not warranted."

"I'm not sure I understand all that."

"You will."

"Do you mean that the feelings I had toward my parents, I impose on strangers?"

"Feelings. And demands."

"I never grew up then."

"That's approximately it."

"I certainly wasn't grown up that time in Florida. I never felt less adult in my life. Everyone had deserted me. Martin wasn't clever enough. Julia was too clever. I couldn't have felt worse if both my arms and legs were cut off."

"In effect they were."

"It's such a lovely day outside I wish I could go for a walk. But that's evading things. Battle. Battle. Every minute here is such a fight. You know, it's hard to relive those moments of feeling so deserted. A human being isn't made to stay by himself."

"An adjusted human being can tell the difference between actual and imagined desertion."

"But it's so hard. I think that night was the beginning of all this mess. I still don't know why I ran up to the man's room. Perhaps I thought there was nothing more to lose with neither Martin nor Julia working to preserve me. It was like a conspiracy, let me tell you. I guess I wanted love so badly that for a moment I thought that sex could take its place." Sue Ellen paused. Her eyebrows came together in thought. "Am I still doing that?"

"Well, are you?"

"Why don't you ever give me a straightforward answer? Yes, that's what I do. I hop into bed with somebody and for a moment I'm secure and loved and important. That sounds pretty stupid, but even to my own ears it sounds true. If they had battled as I wanted them to, I wouldn't have run up to six eleven. That's a hard thing to admit."

Sue Ellen waited, feeling that her mind was about to recall another thought. "There's this to be said, though. I honestly believe that I wanted to take care of myself."

"Why do you say that?"

"I feel it. When I worked in Julia's shop, I didn't try to evade my responsibilities. Maybe I thought it was a last straw or something."

She was already awake when Martin knocked on the door at a quarter to eight. All through the night, sleep had come and gone fitfully. Her body felt dragged out and half alive. She went to the window and stared out at the new day hoping to absorb some of its crisp energy. It would be best to walk into the store looking as though she hadn't a care in the world. Herself a newly risen sun. She felt the coating of stale nicotine in her mouth and, absently, went to the bathroom to pull herself together.

Considerately Julia had brought along her valise last night. She took out a toothbrush and fresh underwear. What mattered now was to be able to forget yesterday. Begin all over. Make a New Year's resolution though it was only April. Resolve to live each day as it came, undaunted.

In half an hour Sue Ellen had reconstructed a presentable person of herself. She got Martin and they went downstairs for a quick breakfast. Then he drove her to the shop, promising to call for her at six.

Julia stood on a small ladder setting rings and necklaces into the window, her nostrils slightly pinched from the musty odor of heat which settled behind the glass.

"Hi." Sue Ellen dropped her purse on a shelf behind one of the counters and went to hand Julia the display boxes.

Tourists slept late on Saturday mornings. The store was empty except for themselves.

"Ready for a tough day?" Julia said.

"Ready for anything."

Julia came down off the ladder and dusted specks from her grey skirt. "Glad you're so cheerful. I worried about you last night."

"Don't do that." She found a cloth and wiped fingerprints from the glass counters. "I haven't a problem in the world."

"You don't say." A hint of amusement lingered in Julia's eyes.

"Well, my biggest problem," Sue Ellen hesitated, unable to meet the woman's scrutiny, "is how to get rid of Martin so we can spend tonight together. Alone."

"Oh, honey, didn't he tell you? We're going out tonight, Martin and myself. I promised to show him the sights. You know how it is." She lit a cigarette and poised it in the groove of a jade ash tray. "Better to play the game. More comfortable, fewer questions. Easier for you."

"And you," she said bitterly. "Going to make love to him too? Kiss him in dark corners so that he's convinced you're a real woman?"

"Sue Ellen, that's unkind. And childish. What would you have me do? Punch him in the nose and drag you off to my cave? Try to be sensible about this. It'll get you much farther." The sternness of her mouth changed to a smile as two women strolled into the store.

Sue Ellen took out a box of earrings and busied herself writing code numbers on their tags while Julia attended to the customers. So that's how it was. Hiding, wearing a mask, being mauled for the sake of respectability. Or maybe she liked Martin. This new possibility came to her with a horrible thud. She could hardly wait until the sale was complete and the women gone.

"Do you like sleeping with men?" Sue Ellen said in a voice suddenly subdued.

"And yourself? Child, does it make any difference?" She took the cloth from Sue Ellen's hand and hooked a pearl choker around her neck. "We should be grateful for whatever little happiness there is. You'll be gone next week. In a month you will have forgotten me. Why should we spend these last days arguing? If I go out with Martin this evening, we can have all day tomorrow. Just the two of us. Compromise is part of the scheme of things."

She wanted to understand. Julia's words were sensible. But all Sue Ellen could imagine was a whole evening alone, stretching in front of her. What was she supposed to do with all those hours? Lock herself up in the room like her mother used to do?

The possibility that she couldn't trust herself to be alone nagged at Sue Ellen all afternoon. She wasn't the type to curl up with a book. Miami was filled with attractive people looking for a good time. If she strolled along the street for fifteen minutes, she could pick up almost anyone she wanted.

As six o'clock approached Sue Ellen pleaded with Julia. "As long as you two are going out, why can't I keep the shop open until ten. There'll be plenty of other stores open in the neighborhood. It'll give me something to do."

Julia's forehead needed fresh powder and it wrinkled in disapproval. Sue Ellen noticed age lines she hadn't seen before. They had spent a hard day and even with the door closed, customers kept trying the handle and peering in.

"You've had enough," Julia said. "You'd probably be mobbed. One girl alone. It's too much."

Sue Ellen knew that the subject was closed. She couldn't sway this woman as she did Martin. "I just thought…"

"Well, don't think. I'm losing money by closing, but for a reason. You."

Thanks, Sue Ellen thought. Thanks for nothing.

Martin arrived promptly at six and drove Sue Ellen back to the hotel. She waited for him to gather up enough nerve to tell her about his date with Julia. They were halfway home before he brought it up.

"You know how it is," he said, though she hadn't asked him for any explanations. "That sort of thing is expected of a man. You wouldn't want her to get any wrong ideas about us, would you?"

"Wouldn't right idea be more like it?" she said.

Sue Ellen put her head back against the seat and gave up trying to make any sense out of these adults. Each going out with the other because it was the right thing to do. Each wanting to be with her but afraid to be found out.

"Have yourselves a ball," Sue Ellen said.

"You'll be all right," Martin said, reassuring himself. "Take dinner and put it on the bill. I'll be home before you count twenty."

"Relax." Sue Ellen opened the door of her room. "This is, after all, your vacation."

She listened to Martin's footsteps fading as he returned along the corridor to the elevator. Then she flung herself into the reading chair and looked at her fingernails. Six thirty. At least five and a half hours before he'd be back. She felt neither tired nor hungry. Unbidden her imagination rummaged through various alternatives for spending the evening. Seldom did she have this kind of freedom. There had always been someone to keep an eye on her. Chattering and laughter floated in from outside. The whole world was going to dinner. Saturday night. A night for fun, for company. She looked at her empty bed, the squat chest of drawers, a line of dust on the rim of the lampshade. Impossible. She couldn't sit here like this for five and a half hours. Jeff was the only person in the world who could do it. And she wasn't Jeff.

Then she picked up the phone and asked for room service. A half hour later she opened the door for the waiter to wheel in a cart filled with dishes. She poured herself tea from the china pot and lifted the metal cover from the turkey platter. For awhile she picked at the food and smoked and decided to think about what to do when school was over.

The telephone again. This time she asked for long distance. Jeff would speak to her willingly, if she wanted to discuss careers.

He answered the ring, sounding surprised but pleased to hear her voice. After the usual how are you's, he told her that Richard was there and would like to say hello. Gladly she spoke with Richard too. Yes, she would certainly be home next week. Of course she would love to see him.

When she cradled the receiver, her wrist watch said that it was hardly eight o'clock. In a reflex movement she slammed out of the room and down the four flights of steps.

But there were lots of people in the lobby and it soothed her. She stood on the third step scanning the men in their dinner jackets, the women in silk brocades and plastic shoes, their hair and wrists aglitter with diamonds. People. Some sat on couches and chairs, others lounged beside pillars. Everyone freshly spruced and still sober. She went outside to the yacht basin and smiled up at a little fat boy in plaid walking shorts. He sat on the flying bridge like Little Lord Fauntleroy, reading a comic book and chewing on a stick of licorice.

The street was crowded with automobiles. Radios blared from them. A horn honked. She followed the sound and met the smile of a fellow in a cowboy hat. He winked. Sue Ellen turned away.

She drifted between the strollers. She bent down for her hand to be licked by a white poodle puppy who had jumped up at the hem of her dress.

"He's lovely," she said to the dowager at the other end of the yellow lead.

The woman pulled her dog away and held him tightly beside her ankle.

Sue Ellen moved on, thinking how nice it would be to have a puppy of her own. The more she thought about it, the more the idea appealed to her. She began paying attention to all the dogs that passed, trying to decide what kind would suit her best. Many blocks later, she found a drug store and went inside to look for pet shops in the classified directory. Maybe she would have the good fortune to find one that was still open.

After unsuccessfully dialing a few, she got a response in a store out at Coral Gables. The man said that he was just about closing now but he would wait for her, if she came right away. Sue Ellen noted his address on a slip of paper and went out to find a cab.

Coral Gables proved to be further away than Sue Ellen had anticipated. She reached the store just as the man was locking up. She was prepared to plead with him to go back inside, but he didn't need to be convinced.

"Sure do look anxious," he said. A straggly mustache stained brown curled down over one side of his lips. He wore Army fatigues held by suspenders. The outfit emphasized his withered age. Only the smile in his eyes retained youth. They were two wells of kindness.

"I never had a dog before," she said, touching her hair back into place. "Guess I am a little excited at the prospect."

They went back inside to the warm animal smell. The place, though dark, was alive with movement. Here and there, a bird scratched the gravel in his cage. Fish swam endlessly between undulating water plants. A parrot rocked from side to side on his perch.

"Have anything special in mind?" the man asked, switching on a porcelain chandelier.

"No. Just something small, I guess. We have an apartment in New York. I don't want to cage some poor beast who should be roaming the hills." Dimly she remembered a black and brown spotted creature with bow legs to whom Clellie threw scraps when he came sniffing.

"Let's see." He unrolled an oilskin pouch and dug a black pipe into the contents. "We have a few little fellas in the back, if you'd care to take a look at them."

She followed his shuffling steps to a series of cages with pups curled among strips of newspaper.

"There's a nice little dachsie there. And a beagle fella there. And them's cocker spaniels. Good heads. You can tell the way the ears set." He opened the door and lifted out a blonde, silky haired puppy. It yawned and tried to nuzzle into the crook of his elbow. "All wormed. Got his first shots, too. Nice flat belly. Healthy dogs, all of 'em."

He set the puppy on the floor and Sue Ellen watched it stagger sleepily, then sit down and yawn again.

"May I pick him up?" She was already kneeling for the animal.

"My pleasure."

The warmth of him gave off a clean doggy odor. He blinked huge brown eyes at Sue Ellen and the tail waggled for a minute. She lifted him close to her face and felt the cold nose against her cheek.

"Yes, I like him. What about food?"

"That's a good dog. I'll give you a regular schedule for him. When you get back home, take the fella to a vet. He'll tell you what to do from there. Or if you're gonna be in Florida for awhile yet, I'll give you the name of a man in Miami."

"Please." The pup rolled himself into a ball and tried to get back to sleep.

They went back to the front of the store. The man took a jar of Pervinal and wrapped it up. "What ever else you feed him, he'll get a spoonful of vitamins every day. Here's the vet's card. Be sure and call on him first thing Monday morning. That'll be sixty dollars all together. If you give me your address, I'll mail you his papers when they come in."

Sue Ellen returned to the hotel elated. She no longer felt alone.

Room service brought her up a raw egg, pablum and warm milk. He took a few laps of it, then waddled back over to her feet, where he sat down and put his head on the toe of her shoe. She picked him up and sat him on her lap. He dug for a second in the material of her skirt and then with a little sigh, was fast asleep.

She sat in the dark with this little bit of life, stroking him and crooning to herself. The world of people forgotten, she felt part of the little dog's contentment.

Martin came in and found her still sitting in the same position. She hadn't thought about time. It was still eight o'clock for all she knew.

"What's all this?" he said, not knowing whether to laugh or be concerned.

"What does it look like?" She put her palm over the pup's face, afraid that the light might wake him.

Martin sat down on the edge of the bed and untied his shoe laces. "Yours?"

"Mine." She didn't care whether he'd had a good time or where they'd gone or what they did.

"Be careful of your dress."

"So what?" She was feeling rather aloof. Nor did she feel like helping Martin to understand the whys and wherefores of the puppy's presence.

"Bought him?" Martin was trying to make conversation.

"Um hmm."

"Name him yet?"

She pursed her lips. "All this talk is just going to wake him up."

"Not on your life. They sleep like maniacs. I used to have a dog when I was a kid. Not half as pretty as that one. He used to go away for weeks at a time. Always up to no good. Tipsy, Pop called him. Looked like a drunken bum." He folded his hands between his knees.

It occurred to Sue Ellen that she didn't know anything about Martin's childhood. She had taken it for granted that he had been born grown up. The concept of Martin in short pants, maybe skinny, slinging books over his shoulder and going to school was a strange idea.

"Sure," he said, reading her thoughts. "I'm a country boy. New Jersey. Oh, it's all built up around there now. But we used to have chestnut trees. Mosquitoes in the summer. You'd have liked it there."

He sounded innocent and boyish. The blue of his eyes seemed to reflect a swimming hole.

"We had mosquitoes in Virginia too," she said. The quick beat of the pup's heart tapped against her hand. She pulled it carefully out and took a cigarette from Martin. "But it wasn't mosquitoes so much as moths. They just covered up the porch lights. How did you ever meet my mother?"

Martin smiled at the question and lay back on the pillow. "Believe it or not," he said, "your mother was quite a gal. She worked for the Red Cross during the first world war. I met her in the states and wrote to her all the time I was overseas. But I guess I wasn't so glamorous afterwards. No uniform, no money. She was the kind of a woman who liked to enjoy herself. Popular. And I was a clerk on Wall Street. It didn't seem fair for me to marry her and make a drudge out of such a pretty thing. So like a dope, I thought we'd wait till I made a little cash. And she got tired of waiting. It wasn't fair of me, I suppose, but after my first wife died I started sending her clippings about me from the Times. One thing led to another. And..."

"And here we are," Sue Ellen murmured.

CHAPTER TWELVE

"It's a funny thing the way the past refuses to stay put. Reminds me of that painting. The way the lines weave in and out. No beginning. No middle. No end."

The soft green air of summer came in through the open windows, bringing with it a taste of soot from the crowded streets. Dr. Ross had set up a table book case on his desk of black wrought iron. It held a dozen or so issues of a psychology journal, giving the room a feeling of movement and growth quite different from the solid, unyielding texts banked into the wall.

"I don't know whether it was the puppy or the way Martin was talking or a combination of the two. But I felt a little sturdier within myself that night. Anyway, I'm glad for Terry. That's what I named him. He was something to take care of. He depended on me. And he saved me many times, not just that night, from making a fool of myself with men." Sue Ellen smiled. "I guessed I liked being motherly."

She let the puppy sleep beside her on the bed and took him along the next day to show Julia. Apparently Julia had done a good job of buttering Martin up because he didn't object at all to Sue Ellen spending the day without him.

Julia pulled up along side the hotel in her Mercedes and Sue Ellen ran down to meet her with the pup hugged securely to her breast. "Isn't he wonderful?" she said as Julia drove away. "Just as good as he can be. No nerves, no vomiting. Practically house broken already."

"Just keep him on *your* lap," Julia chuckled.

Both women were in shorts. Sue Ellen figured they were going to the beach house where they could play on the sand with her dog. Julia seemed in a good humor, smiling behind her sun glasses. The radio played very softly. And she drove at a pleasant thirty five miles an hour. All very placid. Sue Ellen wanted Julia to admire her dog and if possible, be a little jealous. But Julia's good humor seemed impenetrable. Sue Ellen wasn't going to ask about what had happened with Martin. No questions meant an adult acceptance. Julia should approve of that. And besides, she didn't really care. What people did behind her back was their business. She had a private life of her own that nobody knew about. It wasn't exactly the sort of thing to be proud of. But in time she would have good secrets as well as bad ones. When her dog grew up enough to go for walks, they would discover many wonderful things together. That was something to look forward to.

"What did you name him?"

"Martin asked me the same thing last night. I haven't yet. Takes time to find the right one. I have to get to know his personality a little better."

"Good idea."

Each seemed to be waiting for the other to resume a more personal conversation. Sue Ellen wasn't sure that she wanted anything intense to happen today. A new wave of purity and cleanliness had come into her life with the dog. He seemed to be guarding her from evil thoughts. It was like a magic spell. And Sue Ellen felt afraid to break it, lest she be unable to regain this fantastic happiness.

"Where are we going?" she asked casually. Perhaps Julia had dreamed up a party or an afternoon of being outside where neither would be able to touch the other.

"Wherever you'd like."

This was Sue Ellen's opportunity. She tried to recall the advertisements in leaflets. Something about a Seaquarium. "How about treating me like a tourist?" she said lightly.

"Much too early in the day. The bars don't get going for quite a while yet."

Sue Ellen let the misunderstanding slide. Certainly she was in no mood to drink. The stuff didn't agree with her anyway. Besides she didn't want to take the dog into a smoky atmosphere.

"I guess you're not in a mood to be alone with me," Julia said. "Do I bore you already?"

"Don't be ridiculous." It wasn't boredom at all. She had never felt quite so alive. The world was various and wonderful. Yet it felt made out of glass. She felt afraid it might break.

Though Julia talked this way, she didn't sound as though she believed her own words. They drove directly to the beach house and she didn't seem shy about taking Sue Ellen inside.

For a few minutes they watched the puppy scamper around the floor. He had been fed and watered. All was happy in his little world. Julia came up behind Sue Ellen and put her lips against the girl's neck.

"I missed you," she said. "So much."

Sue Ellen stiffened under Julia's caress. She tried to keep her eyes on the puppy. The woman's fingers cupped her waist and moved upward along her ribs. She could feel Julia's breasts pressing against her back. She wanted to pull away but the caressing fingers were fast changing her mind. Why should she hurt Julia's feelings? Only a few more days. Then she'd be safely in New York. If this were going to be a long drawn out relationship, she could feel justified in stopping it now. But just these few days. Hours.

Sue Ellen turned in Julia's arms. Their parted lips met. The pressure of their bodies touching increased. Sue Ellen forgot about the puppy. A sound of lapping surf came in through the half open windows. Her palms felt along the hollow behind Julia's hips.

All good intentions died. In their place came the familiar pulsing desire. Her stomach drew in and she pulled the woman close in her arms.

"It's crazy how I need you," Julia said.

Sue Ellen knew just what she meant. But crazy or not, they needed each other. As they kissed they were walking, almost like a dance, until a couch on the veranda caught them. They fell together onto the couch and they lay close to each other, touching and probing with eager hands, aware of the salt air and rush of the sea.

"I've always wanted it out in the open," Julia said against Sue Ellen's throat. "The sun beating down on bare bodies. A part of nature. Warm beneath a blue sky. Someday I'm going to buy an acre of land and fence it in just for that purpose."

They lay side by side, touching but not rushing their desire. Sue Ellen put her cheek on the woman's blouse and worked her nose into the V neck. She didn't care who saw.

"We'd better go inside," Julia said after awhile. Her breath was shallow, the words clipped. Forcibly she pushed Sue Ellen away, then took her by the wrist and dragged her into the bedroom.

But they didn't reach the bed. They collapsed in one corner of the room and pulled off each other's clothes with impatient fingers.

"I love you," Sue Ellen whispered. She flung herself eagerly against Julia. And she bit the woman's thigh, needing to bruise her. Needing to leave some mark of her presence in the woman's life.

For Sue Ellen knew that this would be the last time for them. The last time and the best. And she gripped the woman firmly, sincerely resolving now that she would never again possess anybody out of wedlock. She would take her fill, storing up satisfaction enough to quiet the craving for perhaps years to come. Her desire flamed insatiably. Her body ached with tension. But she couldn't let go. She couldn't stop. Again and again she demanded fulfillment. Her face had become grim and white with concentration.

"Hey there," Julia said, forcing her away for a minute. "It's not going out of style, you know."

"I want you," Sue Ellen rasped and flung herself against the woman.

It was the whimpering puppy, alone in the next room, that finally brought Sue Ellen back to her senses. Kneeling back away from Julia, she surveyed the bruises on the inside of the woman's thighs. Touching them with her fingertips, she murmured, "You're beautiful." Then, naked, she ran in to the puppy.

He was sitting beside a terry cloth slipper, a string of the material dangling from the side of his mouth. Sue Ellen burst out laughing.

Julia came in to join her. She flopped heavily onto the couch and put her legs up on the arm. "It's a terry cloth eater, eh?" she said with a tired smile. "Cheaper than steaks, anyway."

Sue Ellen looked at the woman's used up body. It was beautiful, indeed. And she would never touch it again.

"I'll call him Terry," she said. "He'll remind me of you."

Sue Ellen did not go back to the shop on Monday. Julia did not phone. And Sue Ellen knew that she understood. Martin drove her to the vet. She spent the next few days fattening Terry up for the trip back to New York.

It was easy enough to avoid sleeping with Martin. Her company was sufficient for him. They shared boat rides and little trips around the city. Each felt an unconscious lightness now that the episode with Julia had ended.

Sue Ellen was looking forward to getting back home. She had a long list of supplies to purchase. Terry needed his own bed and dishes. She wanted to buy a black leather collar and rubber bones. They had to get a travelling case so he could ride with them on the plane.

Martin said, "How about rompers?"

But Sue Ellen didn't think it very funny.

New York was still piled high with snow when they returned. It was a bleak world. Automobiles smothered beneath drifts, sidewalks scattered with ashes emphasized the wondrous playland of

Florida. Sue Ellen went into the apartment and snuggled up to the radiator. Terry wiggled out of her arms and tottered over to Jeff.

"He's a nifty," Jeff said.

Sue Ellen felt a sting of jealousy as she watched Terry obviously enjoying a masculine playmate. She knew that dogs preferred men to women. It didn't seem fair. But she comforted herself with the thought that Jeff would be going back to law school the day after tomorrow.

Every time she saw Jeff, he looked steadier, more conservative. He had taken to wearing vests with a gold watch chain. She wondered if there was any fun in his life. But she didn't have the courage to ask.

Sue Ellen went back to school. Thanks to Terry, her life had a settled feeling approaching normalcy. Her mind was free to study or to consider what kind of gown to have made for the Prom.

She paid for two tickets to the dance and then realized there wasn't anyone around she would care to go with. Martin would look out of place. Jeff could hardly dance and he might not want to be bothered with such foolishness. It was a real problem.

Mentally she went down the list of males in her life and paused when she came to Richard. She remembered the long distance phone conversation. Obviously he liked her. There was no reason for her not to invite him. She phoned.

It was gratifying to hear the pleasure with which he accepted. Yes, she liked Richard. He treated her with respect. The novelty of it made her feel respectable. She decided to cultivate Richard and have for herself a normal, conventional relationship.

Sue Ellen made him take her ice skating and to the theater. They went to parties at the homes of other people their own age. He brought her orchids and she thrilled at the gesture. Sometimes they drove up to Connecticut for an afternoon and took dinner at a countryside restaurant. She would let him kiss her good night, but only at such times when she could close the door quickly and safely between them.

Spring touched the air again with its colorful hand. She stared out the school room window and counted the days until all this nonsense would be over. Terry had outgrown his collar. The world had moulted and everything felt new and promising. Except for one nagging thought in the back of her mind, Sue Ellen's world would have been perfect. She decided at last to see a doctor.

Three consecutive pregnancy tests proved negative but still she didn't believe them. Sue Ellen went to another doctor and took three more. Only grudgingly did she accept their similar verdict. It almost seemed as though she wanted to be pregnant. The idea fascinated her with its horror. Her life would be ruined. Martin's reputation smashed. The thought of abortion did not enter her mind.

But really there was nothing to think about. Strain and worry and overwork had caused this delay in her feminine cycle. It happened frequently, both doctors told her. And yet she couldn't rid her mind of the crazy notion that somehow she had managed to fool them. Nothing could really convince her that an embryo was not growing in her womb.

On the surface, however, she remained carefree. She strolled along Fifth Avenue with Richard and they stopped to look in windows. He had a way of touching her forearm that seemed to protect her. And when she spoke, he always listened carefully.

One night they paused at J. & J. Sloane. A beautiful dining room grouping stood in the window. "When I get married," Sue Ellen said, "I'm not going to have a formal dining room."

"All right," he said. "I don't think your husband will object to anything you want to do."

Sue Ellen felt very confident. For two months she had been on good behavior. Frankly she was curious to linger with Richard and discover how his hands would understand a woman. And supposing she was pregnant, after all. A woman with child needs a husband.

"You're a very promising man," she murmured.

She led him uptown to the Fifty Ninth Street circle. They would go for a ride in a hansom through Central Park. Alone in the dark intimacy of the carriage, he would not be able to resist her.

A number of carriages stood lined up near the Park's entrance. Bored drivers sat holding limp whips. She patted a horse's nose and looked at Richard.

"Would you like to go for a ride?" he asked.

He was satisfyingly easy to handle. "I'd love it," she answered.

Richard helped her inside. The hood of the carriage folded back so they could see the stars. But it sat at an angle calculated to keep everything but those stars from being able to watch them.

"It's chilly," she said and watched Richard pull the carriage robe up over their knees.

His black hair shone with its natural polish. She wanted to touch his hair with her lips. The two months of good behavior seemed like centuries. She let her hand fall side ways off her lap and their fingers touched beneath the covers.

"I remember," she said, "you were the only boy who really cared about my feelings that day on the beach."

"I still do," he said.

She knew this was so. He had a sensitive face which could betray the smallest lie. Richard did care. And he had never tried to touch her that way, so she could trust what he said. Maybe he had never, ever gone to bed with a woman. The idea of being his first thrilled her. She could train him. He would come to her like an angel and she would show him how devils behaved. With his new knowledge, Richard would be tied to her forever. He would worship her, give her anything. She would be the foundation of his existence. And he would never want to betray her. Unconsciously she moved closer to him. Their legs touched.

"You're the only man in the world I really trust," she whispered to him.

Their faces were so close that when the carriage jolted, neither could tell who kissed the other. But Sue Ellen knew. She let her mouth cling to his until he put his arms around her. Carefully one of her hands slid up the back of his neck. She held his head and kept her lips pressed insistently to his. Gradually the rest of their bodies began to touch. She made her breasts flatten out against his jacket. The throbbing ache in her legs told Sue Ellen that she had passed the point of no return. She must have him possess her. Richard must be all her own. She took his hand and lifted it to her bosom.

"Whatever you do, I trust it," she repeated. Slowly she stroked his thigh as the clip clop of the horse's hooves covered her words.

Instinctively she knew that in order to have Richard, he must propose to her. He was not the sort of man to respect a woman who would let him go all the way without a marriage ring. And, for her own piece of mind, she wanted to get married. It was becoming too wearing on her nerves to abstain. And having a husband was the most sensible way out of her dilemma.

"I love you," Richard said. The simple words were an inevitable climax to the romantic ride beside the dark and rustling trees.

"Oh darling, I've waited so long." And in a particular sense, her words were quite sincere.

Sue Ellen got out of the carriage with a new feeling of vitality. She put her arm through his and walked beside the park. With every step she waited for him to suggest that they go some place to be alone.

And Richard spoke about the job he would take in his father's firm. He could finish his course in business administration during the evenings. Money was no problem. It was completely beside the point to her that he mentioned it at all. Even if Richard were a pauper, she knew that Martin would contribute. Martin wouldn't want an illegitimate child on his hands. He would be very glad when she told him about her forthcoming marriage. He would thank her for being so considerate and adult.

CHAPTER THIRTEEN

"That idea of being pregnant really came in handy." Sue Ellen smiled to herself with realization. "Any other girl in my place would have been thankful for the first doctor's verdict. I was disappointed. And I needed the excuse. Because if I wasn't pregnant, Martin would have been a problem. And most of all I wouldn't have been able to excuse myself for forcing a quick marriage. Let's face it, doctor. I couldn't wait. I needed to get Richard horizontal. Any man, I suppose, would have served the purpose. But marriage was my obsession, my goal. Marriage I could hide behind, do anything I wanted. Poor Richard."

They had the wedding planned for August. Even so Sue Ellen begruded the two months. Sixty days more of sleeping alone. It was a big pill to swallow. But she kept telling herself how good it would be. And she felt very proud to control herself for that long. It would make four months altogether. A world's record, no doubt.

She busied herself with going apartment hunting. Martin wanted to go with her and share these last few hours of being together. In a perverse way he was looking forward to the promised birth of their son. It would prove him still a young man. It would deny the loneliness facing him and make up in part for being separated from Sue Ellen. Neither of them worried about explaining the premature birth to Richard. Sue Ellen could handle that when the time came and they both knew it.

So she read the apartment section and phone real estate brokers. Anything she wanted, Richard was glad for her to get. As long as she was happy, he was happy. She visited pent houses and duplex apartments overlooking the East River.

But they were all too large. She wanted something cozy. An apartment to hug close when she would have to stay there alone. Wishfully she considered making Richard stay home with her. But that would be utterly impossible and she thrust the thought from her mind.

At last she found a six room apartment on Sutton Place and called Richard to sign the two year lease. School prevented them from taking an extended honeymoon. She could have talked Richard out of going to summer school but the honeymoon didn't make that much of a difference to her. So long as she could have him, it didn't matter where.

It was to be a small wedding with just the immediate families. Martin had arranged this at her request. She didn't want it to be glaringly obvious to four hundred people that her mother wasn't present.

In a fit of sudden confidence, she sent an invitation to her father. She didn't dare think about whether he would reply or attend. She simply needed to make the gesture for old time's sake.

As the wedding day approached, Richard became increasingly attentive. He took liberties with her body which Sue Ellen accepted as though it were the first experience of her life. Little did he know that it was she who finagled moments alone with him where no one could see. She touched him intimately, pretending it was accidental. And Richard responded with a candor and enjoyment that promised wonderful satisfaction after the legalities were performed.

Frankly Sue Ellen was glad to have the sanction of law for a change. Her conscience could rest in peace. She thought her demands were no more fervent than any other red blooded woman. Altogether, she felt very proud and relieved that her difficulties could be so easily solved.

The morning mail brought a letter post marked Virginia. Her heart jolted as she scanned the type written characters and she picked up Terry for support, holding him on her lap as she tore open the flap.

Inside was the RSVP card. On the bottom was typed: Of course I'll be there. Thank you for remembering.

She pulled Terry close to her and he looked into her face inquiringly. Her hands trembled as she stroked his ears. He reached up and licked the salt tears from her cheek.

The days passed and all she could think of was what he would look like. Perhaps she wouldn't recognize him and that would be terrible. He couldn't possibly know her. What had she in common with the little girl wearing metal barrets across her pigtails?

Martin kept telling her it would be all right. Perhaps he had a good reason for not answering her other letters. And when Martin stopped reassuring her, Richard took over. Between the two of them, they managed to calm Sue Ellen so she could live until the day of his arrival.

And then it was time. Richard's parents and Martin and her father were all to meet in her house at nine o'clock. The minister would arrive at ten and after the ceremony, breakfast at the Hotel Pierre.

Richard Bower Sr. and his wife both loved Sue Ellen like a daughter. Mrs. Bower had never forgotten the episode of her sweet sixteen party. She was bound and determined to be a second mother to the girl. Sue Ellen knew this and did not resist her affections. The matronly chest was comforting to lean against in moments of need.

But now Sue Ellen could just about manage to greet them civilly. She kept listening for the door bell, her face tense, unable to smile. Maybe he wouldn't show up after all.

"Of course he'll be here," Mrs. Bower said, waving a coffee colored lace handkerchief. "Parents always love their children, no matter what."

And then Martin was opening the door to a lean man whose face was sunburnt and leathery. Not a sparkle of color had drained from his hair. The shoulders stooped a bit but it was not from the excesses of drink. He wore a serge suit, obviously new, and all of his long limbs were steady.

As Sue Ellen looked at him approaching, the room began to swim. Flashes of hot and cold chased alternately through her. She blinked to steady herself. As she swayed forward, her father's arms went around her.

She clung to his neck, wanting never to let go. "Oh, Daddy...Daddy." She felt him patting her back.

"I guess you're just the same as always, little brat." But his voice wasn't any steadier than hers.

She held on tight, her eyes shut so that the world would disappear, leaving just the two of them. She rubbed her cheek against his, hoping to feel the scraggle of beard. But in her honor it had been shaved clean and she could smell the faint dusting of powder.

"I couldn't believe it when you sent the card back. After all my letters. ... I just couldn't believe it."

"You say letters?"

"Yes. Lots of them, especially at first."

She heard her father sigh tiredly. "I don't suppose you were big enough to mail them yourself."

"Of course not. I gave them to mother."

A moment of clarity put everything in place.

"The most important letter got to me anyway," he said. "Now, why don't you introduce me to your future husband and all those fine people?"

Sue Ellen became conscious of everyone looking at them. Mrs. Bower was wiping her own eyes and trying very hard to smile. The gesture only emphasized her pointed chin and the fact that her dentures didn't fit too well.

Gladly Sue Ellen took her father around, showing him off. She held him possessively around the waist as though somebody was bound to snatch him away.

Richard became suddenly unimportant. All she wanted was to go into another room and hear every minute of what her father had been doing all these years.

But she couldn't escape with him. Everyone descended and captured them. Richard said, "Pleased to meet you, sir." Martin shook hands with a sportsmanlike attitude.

It was very strange indeed when the minister arrived. Sue Ellen had completely forgotten what he was supposed to do here. The last thing on earth she wanted right now was to be married. Snatched away from her father just when she had him again. She wondered if he shared the feeling. But his wide set eyes betrayed nothing except pleasure at the prospect of witnessing his daughter's marriage.

Sue Ellen went through with the ceremony, her mind forming all kinds of traps to prevent her father from going back South. The idea that he might come live with them for awhile presented itself. She knew he wouldn't accept, but what was to prevent her from trying?

The Biblical words droned on, unattended. She could gaze beyond Mrs. Bower's corsage to the aquiline nose set above the firm mouth. He looked so well cared for. There must be a woman in his life. Perhaps he had remarried and brought her to live in the old house. Maybe there was a little girl who slept in her old room. These questions plagued her, as she lifted her hand for Richard to slip on the plain gold wedding band.

"With this ring, I thee wed."

And somehow it was complete. She leaned her face forward for Richard's kiss. Someone else kissed her and someone else. Her father finally came up. He held her by the arms so that she could not fling them around his neck again and kissed her gently on the forehead.

"How long are you going to be in New York?"

"Till this afternoon."

"But you can't go. Not yet. Not before we've talked."

"You've got a few other things, far more important." His smile was the same unyielding smile she had learned to respect.

"I'll never see you again," she said, as though Fate had decreed impending death for one of them.

CHAPTER FOURTEEN

"As I look back at that moment, it wasn't sadness that I really felt. It was anger. You know, I had expected my father to be a worn out, disappointed old man, bent with grieving and loneliness. I couldn't stand to see such tangible proof of how well he had managed without me. Of course, I couldn't take it out on him directly though. How could I? The only person I ever really loved ...." Sue Ellen paused, battling with herself to find a more precise truth. "Anyway, I believed I loved him. And brazenly I wished he could come live with me instead of Richard. How's that for honesty?"

Dr. Ross's pen moved quickly over the paper. "You have a good insight into yourself," he said.

Sue Ellen hardly touched a thing at the wedding breakfast. She drank cups of black coffee in an effort to steady herself. Soon it would be her duty to go away with Richard. This thought, so desirable last week, became frightening to her now. She felt stifled and choking, like an animal locked in a cage. If anyone noticed her discomfort, they were polite enough to overlook it. Only natural for a bride to be nervous. Richard wasn't eating very well either. So the two of them made a charming, devoted looking couple.

She watched her father chatting amiably with Mr. Bower and Martin, just as though he were around every day of the year.

Richard bent his head close to hers. "Are you all right?"

"I'm too happy, darling."

At least someone cared. Yet she wanted to push his sweet face into the fruit cup.

The waiters took away and brought more courses. She couldn't see how these people could eat so much. But they continued to pack it away. There was nothing she could do except wait until Richard could take her irrevocably for his own. In some small way, this thought comforted her. She was Richard's responsibility. She belonged to him. Her position as the junior Mrs. Bower was something nobody could take away. Mothers, fathers, lovers, they could drift in and out of one's life. But a husband had to be there always.

She touched Richard's sleeve. "Do you think we can go soon?"

He nodded.

Yes, gratifying that Richard really wanted her. She glanced at her father paying a gentlemanly compliment to Mrs. Bower. You'll be sorry, she thought. Mentally she broke in two the precious bond between them.

Then everyone was having a last cup of coffee and she and Richard were striding swiftly out of the hotel, past the blue canopy and into the limousine. They were to spend their honeymoon week in the Bower cabin in Maine. Richard wanted to be alone with her amongst the quiet pine. No people, no dressing for dinner. Just the two of them ... getting better acquainted.

She stretched out in the spacious back seat and watched New York roll away behind them.

"Maybe we should have flown," Richard said in a self-conscious tone. "Ten hours. It's a long time."

"We still can." She looked at him sitting all the way over at the other window. He looked very young and a little afraid. "But then again, I've never really seen the New England countryside."

She didn't give a darn about the countryside. But it was an appropriate remark. Shy and ladylike. She must remember her role at all times. The contrast between this and their bed life would make Richard appreciate her all the more.

This struck her as a splendid idea but as they rode along upstate, Sue Ellen became impatient. They were legally married. Why did he have to sit all the way on the other side of the car like this? She heard only vaguely his comments on the Bower Company's financial outlook for the coming year.

"Dad wants me to take over the vice presidency as soon as I graduate," he was saying. "But I think it would be better for me to feel my way around for awhile."

"Of course. You know best, darling." If he wanted to do any feeling, there she was, ready to be felt. Business be damned. His long legs were crossed at the ankles and the tip of one black shoe wiggled impatiently. He really couldn't be thinking about the Bower Company at a time like this.

Sue Ellen moved over and rested her head on his shoulder. The odor of rich pasture land invigorated her with a desire to be animal. Cows grazing placidly among the green hills made her think of the barn at night. The roar of a bull as he mounted a heifer.

"Would you like to open your collar?" she said. Maybe the formal attire was inhibiting him.

Instead of waiting for Richard to respond, she reached up and undid the button. She let her hand glide upward and mess his hair so that a lock of it fell down on his forehead.

Richard chuckled. He put his arm around her. "You're a wild little thing, aren't you?"

Little? Yes, she felt little beside him. How delicious it was going to be, feeling the strength of him suddenly freed against her.

Without coaxing her mind began to move in phantasy of their promised embrace. It was all right to think about it any way she wanted to. The seal of social approval stripped her imagination of all inhibiting restraint.

They passed a roadside inn. Richard took the speaker and told their chauffeur to stop at the next nice place.

They sent the man inside to freshen up and Sue Ellen made Richard kiss her now that they were alone. Her lips parted his. Their tongues touched. Her nails went into his jacket and clawed down along his back. She wanted to reach underneath and pull the shirt out of his trousers so she could feel his flesh. But he took her hands and held them.

"We can wait," his whispered. "A whole lifetime. Just us. I want to live to see your hair turn. And we'll sit by the fire waiting for our grandchildren to come for Christmas dinner. Maybe I'll be able to play Santa Claus without a pillow beneath my jacket. It's going to be a marvelous life, my dearest. I promise you." He brought her hand up to his lips and touched it with a gentle adoration.

"Yes, we can wait," she said, pushing her knee between the two of his. Actually she wanted to wait. But the sun wasn't even down beneath the horizon yet. They had hours to go. She felt like a person nearly starved to death looking through a glass window at a feast. She could control herself if it weren't for the tantalizing images.

The chauffeur returned. He was young enough to drive faster than he drove, Sue Ellen thought.

She picked up the speaker. "You can do the speed limit, Humphrey."

Pained, Richard looked at her. The dark eyes seemed like a troubled child's. "That wasn't discreet," he said.

"But we're married!"

"Humphrey knows that."

A silence put distance between them. She didn't want Richard to be displeased. She couldn't chance him thinking about anything but her waiting body. Otherwise, he might putter around the cabin. Fix drinks. Take a bath. Maybe even a nap. Richard liked everything to be just so. She had no illusions of changing him so that he would notice. The process would have to be one of gradual training. She must lure his mind away from finances, away from grooming, to the one central core of importance. Her life would be devoted to the purpose of possessing him. She would possess him so completely that even his soul would flow into her. Her desires would become his desires. They would mingle into a single unit of being so that nothing Richard did might exclude her.

"I'm sorry," Sue Ellen whispered. "Perhaps I love you too much." A remorseful smile tilted her lips pathetically downward. "You'll have to teach me not to love you."

"I wouldn't want to do that."

She saw that he was sincerely remorseful in return. His arm moved back around her shoulder.

"If you ever stopped loving me..." The profound horror of this thought made him unable to complete the sentence.

She squeezed his hand. "It's all up to you, I think. Because inside of me I feel that I was created for your love. Only you."

How Sue Ellen wanted to believe her own words. They sounded so beautiful. And if they were true, she could have a marvelous life, free of nightmares. And, in part, it was up to Richard. If he had the good sense to respect her needs, to fulfill them adequately, there was no reason why they couldn't be happy together.

A cloak of darkness was beginning to roll up over the curving sky. The infinite sadness of summer filled her with a nostalgia. In years to come, they would be remembering this moment. This lovely youth. Two resilient bodies capable of germinating a third. Two unlined bodies capable of troves of passion. Someday she would touch Richard and find that he could not respond. And she would recall this ride and the previous moments slipping by, scattered like bottomless riches.

"Hug me tight," she said and her voice trembled. "Please."

Richard laughed. "You're supposed to be happy today."

Headlights of automobiles rushed toward them and swept past. She snuggled up to him in the darkness, oblivious of all protest.

"We'll be there in a few minutes," he said. "Look, you can see the forest over there behind town."

Sue Ellen looked and bit her lips and waited.

Finally they pulled up in front of a log cabin. It nestled beside a lake where two row boats lay, hulls skyward, beside the dock. A fierce coolness of pine plucked at Sue Ellen's nerves. She recalled what Julia had said about being a part of nature. With a last grappling of strength, she waited until Humphrey drove himself off to town for the night.

They stood on the striped Indian rug and looked at each other mutely. A moose head stared from one pine wall.

"There's food in the kitchen. I can fix you a sandwich if you'd like," Richard said. His olive skin held a slight glow of pink.

Sue Ellen didn't even bother to answer. She walked over to her man, put her arms around his waist and pulled him tightly to her.

"Love me," she said. "Just love me."

Humphrey had started a fire in the hearth. The flames crackled and sent a warm, smoky odor toward them.

She let her hands clutch the slimness of his hips. All these months she had been dreaming of this moment. She took his hands and put them on her buttocks. She felt his fingers begin to move, to search along the backs of her thighs.

"I love you," she said and bit into his lip. "Love you … love you."

With eyes closed she undressed him, letting the knowledge of his body come to her through her fingertips. She tugged open his belt.

"I'll do that," he said. He turned away from her to take off his trousers.

She took barely a second to pull off all her own clothes. She dragged him down with her onto the soft rug, embracing him with her legs.

Almost before he touched her, Sue Ellen knew her moment of completion.

Yet, after the months of abstinence, the sleepless nights alone in her empty bed, the one fulfillment was not enough. She wanted him to need her as she needed him. To love her until the aching desire had been quieted completely.

She squeezed him tightly to her with her knees, holding him prisoner within.

His body surged against her.

The heels of her palms slid along the perspiration on his back. An elbow banged into the rug. She wanted him to hurt her, wanted his maleness to tear through her and fill her completely.

Yet in a moment he lay still on top of her, his breathing shallow, his face contorted with ecstatic agony.

She couldn't let him go now, couldn't let him leave her like this. Her head throbbed with the dismal sense of her frustration. He had ceased in the middle of her growing desire.

She tried again and again to force him to respond. The perspiration streamed from her body and soaked into the rug. Yet she knew it was no use.

A sob tore at her throat and she swallowed hard to control it. Her fingernails clawed at the flesh of his shoulders. She needed him, she loved him, she hated him. And she knew that he must satisfy her now or she would surely lose her mind.

She put her hands over his ears and began forcing him down. Marriage made anything all right.

Finally she sighed and put her head into his armpit. "I do love you," she murmured.

"Was it ... all right?"

"Perfect, darling. Just perfect."

She heard his breath expel in a long sigh of relief. No doubt he had been afraid to overestimate his prowess. She must give him confidence. Make him glad to show himself off this way. Not

diamonds or emeralds or mink stoles, but the gift of his physical-
ity would keep her happy.

"There's nothing I'll ever want," she said, "more than what
you've given me tonight."

Richard cleared his throat. "I think we should get dressed."

She watched him don corduroy slacks from the suitcase.
He was still shy about their nakedness. To please him, Sue
Ellen put on a white turtle neck and a pair of black slacks.
She had a lot of training to do but the prospect was far from
unpleasant.

That night she lay in Richard's arms and listened to his gentle
satisfied snoring. They had gone to sleep without anything else
taking place first. It was wiser not to push him, she thought.
Mustn't take the chance of shocking Richard. As long as he
believed that what they did was right and normal, she would have
a willing partner. But he must never begin to question or think
her unduly abandoned. Gradually, as the weeks would go by, she
would increase their meetings, until she knew the dimensions of
her own needing. What Richard wanted didn't matter. He must
be the reflection of her own desire.

For awhile she listened to the trees playing with the wind.
And then she fell asleep, confident that all would work itself out
to her satisfaction.

The next day they went swimming and lay on the raft in
the middle of the lake. She had not approached him before
they'd dressed and now she considered whether or not it would
be permssible for her to touch him where it counted. Deciding
against it, she lay on her back and hummed a soft melody,
attempting to listen to his plans for where their children would
go to college.

Often during the week he spoke about their children. He
looked forward to being an attentive father. Sue Ellen looked at
the flatness of her belly. She believed now that the doctors were
right. If Martin asked about his child, she could get out of the

situation easily enough. Safely married she didn't have to worry about Martin any more. She laughed aloud.

The fact that Richard wanted children so badly was a point in her favor. She always remembered to mention it before they went to bed at night. It proved a legitimate impetus.

The week flew. Sue Ellen counted eleven opportunities during which she might have become with child. She couldn't envision herself as a mother. Or more precisely she couldn't see her figure swelling out so that she would have to wear maternity dresses and waddle down the street like an old dog. But she dared not talk to Richard about precautions. And maybe, if she did have a child, it would give her another interest in life.

They returned to New York and happily Sue Ellen began fixing up their apartment. She finished the living room in black and gold, the bedroom in blue and gold, the kitchen in rust and green and gold. Richard's den became a mahogany atmosphere but she was sure to include a sizeable couch. But not the cleverest eye could tell that she had assured a seductive corner in every room of the apartment.

Once again she went to the doctor for a pregnancy test and once again, he assured her that it was negative.

"Making a baby is not as easy as people believe," he told her.

Well, she was in no rush.

There was plenty to take up her time when Richard was at the office during the day. Mrs. Bower took her around to charity organizations and to her private corsetiere. She showed Sue Ellen albums of Richard's baby pictures.

But when he went to school at night, time became a bore. Good naturedly, Martin spent a few evenings with her.

"Are you happy?" he said.

"Of course, Martin." She had no reason not to be happy. It was only natural that a wife should want to see her husband after a day's work.

"I mean, does he spend enough time with you?"

Martin had made himself at home and was pouring his third Scotch. His chest had begun to sag just a little, as though he spent too many hours sitting in the wing chair.

"I know what you mean," Sue Ellen retorted coldly. She didn't feel cold toward Martin but any sign of affection, no matter how well intentioned, might rouse him to something she did not want.

"Sorry," he reneged, crinkling the cellophane off a cigar. "It's not easy, giving you up."

He sounded sorrier for himself than for embarrassing her. There were plenty of women. He didn't have to cling. And besides, if he'd really wanted her, he could have offered marriage when she'd told him about the child.

The next time Martin phoned, Sue Ellen told him that she had a previous appointment.

CHAPTER FIFTEEN

"For the next year or so, Richard kept me comparatively satisfied. I kept promising him children and he kept trying to help me fulfill that promise. I don't think I abused him. Once a night, sometimes twice. Is that too much? Besides, he learned to hold back so that I could have as much as I needed without tiring him." Sue Ellen felt her lips become try. "I tell you it was fine until he became impatient about having children. This time when I went to the doctor, I was really scared. There's something wrong. I don't know the medical terms. But it prevents me from conceiving. I should have known that my good fortune all those years wasn't just an accident. Anyway, how could I go home and tell this to Richard?"

Sue Ellen came out of the doctor's office. The world felt as though it had fallen away beneath her feet. The sky was a grey veil pierced here and there by the spires of the Empire State Building, the Chrysler Building and all the other pinnacles of finance which could not contribute a single penny toward helping Sue Ellen out of her trouble.

She watched cars and taxis honking each other slowly through cross town traffic. She felt hypnotized. A cardboard woman in a cardboard dream. Sterile. She, of all people in the world, incapable of producing children. The poorest, the most ignorant did it all the time without thinking. And she, who had all the advantages, must remain barren.

A clock in a barber shop said five thirty. She should go home and prepare supper. But the thought of facing Richard chided her. She had never learned to face catastrophe. Someone had always been around to protect her. But this catastrophe she must carry within herself, forever. Of course, she didn't have to tell Richard immediately. But how could he miss seeing it? If ever she had a reason to take a drink, this was it.

She crossed the street and told Humphrey to take the car home. For a while she walked, letting the wind tug open the cashmere coat beneath its belted waistline. Then for no reason at all she hailed a cab.

The driver glanced at her in the rear view mirror. "Where to, lady?"

"Take me to the darkest bar you can find," she said, letting her chin sink beneath the upturned lapels.

"Uptown, honey, or downtown?"

"I don't care."

"There's a nice little spot off Bleecker Street. And you don't have to worry about being treated too rough."

Sue Ellen laughed bitterly. She would never have to worry about being treated too rough. They rode past Washington Square and she saw withered leaves dangling and swinging in the wind.

"Have one for me, will ya?" he said as she paid the fare.

It didn't much matter what kind of a bar she went into. She walked a few steps and pushed open the doors of the first one that presented itself.

The heavy stench of beer greeted her nostrils. She pushed her way through the bar flies and found a booth in the rear. Her mind had yet to absorb the full dimensions of its new information. She pulled her gloves off and dropped them on the knicked table top, trying to fathom the consequences of being childless. Perhaps all the sexual activity in her younger days had ruined her body.

"Scotch," she told the waiter and piled her scarf onto the coat beside her.

She finished one and then two more straight shots. She hadn't eaten anything since noon. The liquor hit her belly hard. The burning sensation hurt but it did not mask the other, greater hurt. A fourth and fifth Scotch followed. Her thought processes began to stagger. She blinked across to the people crowded at the bar. Men stood with woolen shawls draped over them in what was supposed to be a continental fashion.

Men. Men indeed. Maybe it was Richard's fault. Maybe he had hurt her in some way. But he wouldn't understand that. She knew what he would do. He would stand back and accuse her of being incompetent. Then he would ask for a divorce.

He couldn't leave her alone in that big apartment. She couldn't sleep by herself in an empty bed. Richard would hate her and go away. What would she do all alone? Who would want her?

She licked her lips, feeling a queeziness in her stomach. She motioned for the waiter and asked him where the ladies' room was. Holding onto the wall, she made her way to the cubicle. She clung to the sink and felt her belly heave.

A voice said, "Tough drinking on an empty stomach."

Sue Ellen's eyes were tearing as she looked up. The woman had lots of blonde curling hair that poked out stiffly from years of bleaching.

"Oh God," Sue Ellen groaned, feeling another convulsion coming on.

The woman tore off a piece of paper towelling, put it under the cold water tap, then plastered it against Sue Ellen's forehead.

"Yeah, I know how it is," she said philosophically. "But now I got a few contacts and at least the meals come in regular."

Sue Ellen tried to steady herself. The woman had round eyes, made rounder by dark pencilled lids. They gave her an expression of forced laughter which did not quite hide the anguish rising from deep inside. This was a person who lived with misery and took it for granted.

"You look like a clean sort of kid," the woman continued.

"Sure," Sue Ellen grunted. "That's why I'm here like this."

"Well, baby, that's the breaks. Feelin' a little better?"

"Yes, thank you." Her vision began to clear and she saw that the woman couldn't be more than five years older than herself. A great wave of sympathy for this poor creature welled and the tears came, unbidden.

"Oh. Now, now. There's always another guy with a buck in his pocket and a stiff in his pants. Why don't you comb your hair and go see what's doin'?"

The suggestion startled Sue Ellen. A weak hope began to glimmer. Maybe, by some accident, another man could make her pregnant?

"That's the idea, honey. Smile a little. You've got such a pretty face. I used to have a pretty face too, when I was your age." She patted Sue Ellen's cheek. "Just keep rememberin' that smile."

They walked out together. Sue Ellen didn't need anyone to bolster her nerve. She could just as easily have died right then, for all the difference her life made. She went back to her table and leaned her chin on the heel of her palm. She always had to coax Richard to make love to her. A stranger wouldn't need coaxing.

She watched the blonde woman put her wide behind on a bar stool and shake a head up on her stale glass of beer. Occasionally the woman turned around to see how she was doing. And finally she beckoned for Sue Ellen to join her.

Without hesitation Sue Ellen went up to the tired but maternal looking woman.

"Me and Jack here's been thinkin' about makin' us a party. No money, you understand. We're friends. But I know he's got some beans and bacon. I put 'em there myself. How's about it, kiddie? Would you like to join?"

Sue Ellen looked at Jack. He wore a merchant marine watch cap and sweater which seemed to emphasize the horn rimmed glasses and the fact that he'd probably never been further than Coney Island. Jack smoked a pipe with a bent stem. He was trying very hard to be a bruiser. It amused Sue Ellen to think that this skinny guy considered himself capable of handling one woman, let alone two. But the proposition took her mind off herself.

"I'd like that," she said.

"Finish your beer, Charlotte," Jack said. He took off his cap, smoothed back the long brown hair and set the cap back at a jauntier angle. He wiped his lips with a very clean handkerchief.

Both Sue Ellen and Charlotte were taller than he. This didn't seem to bother him. Sue Ellen got her coat and he took each woman by the elbow and led them out of the bar.

Jack lived only two blocks away in a tiny flat with maroon curtains to block out any light that threatened entrance. A cat odor from the hall seeped inside. Jack turned on an old fashioned Emerson which stood in a solid cabinet between the two windows.

"You one of the college kids?" he asked as Charlotte found a can opener and began its squeeking motion around the rim of beans and bacon.

"No. Just a drifter," she said.

"We'll have some more beer."

"Let her eat something first," Charlotte interrupted. The flowered apron tied over her sleezy crepe dress seemed a pathetic attempt at hospitality.

But Sue Ellen took the beer anyway. She didn't want to be sober or aware that she existed. Charlotte brought her the plateful and she watched the beans slop down from the heaping pyramid into a flat mass.

She ate without tasting, knowing that if she could taste it, the mess would not go down.

"Aren't you going to join me?" she asked, noting Charlotte and Jack watching her silently.

"Naw, honey. We just filled up an hour ago."

The words rang with so little truth that Sue Ellen had to turn away in shame. She wondered why these people had befriended her. Couldn't they tell by her clothes that she had money? She took a few swallows from the beer can to wash away the greasty taste and then fell backward on the cot.

"You know," Jack said, rubbing his nostrils with the back of a forefinger. "I think your little friend here would like Maxie Freedman."

"Anybody you say," Sue Ellen put in. "Call up anybody. Anybody." She let her arms flop out sideways on the blanket. Her head rolled to one side. The new short haircut curled into one ear.

"She's a real cutie," Jack said to himself. "Freedman sure would go for you. I guess you do all kinds of tricks, don't you, kid?"

"You name it."

Charlotte said, "But make sure you don't have to puke when he's around. Mr. Freedman has class."

Jack went to the telephone with Charlotte standing at his shoulder. The conversation took but a few minutes. And another few minutes later, a little stout man with not a hair on his head was seated on the blanket beside her.

She brought her glance upward from the plump pink fingers to the shiny, rosy cheeks. He looked packed with vitamins. "Hello, Maxie," she said.

"Hello, sweetheart." He wore a carnation in his lapel and a pearl stickpin which made him look like someone out of a 1920 movie.

Jack had disappeared but Charlotte was sitting on the pillow beside Sue Ellen's head. She could hear the rustle of her undergarments against the crepe.

"Mr. Freedman is a very strong person," Charlotte was saying. As she spoke, her fingers stroked Sue Ellen's forehead. "Some men have trouble enough with one woman. He's a regular Charles Atlas, Mr. Freedman is. And don't I know." Sue Ellen listened to the voice, trained to sound so thrilled and pleased.

"It's good living," Maxie said. "Regular hours, the proper diet. A man doesn't have to lose his virility when he turns thirty-one."

They were all talking as though this were an ordinary evening get together. The only difference was that her body was being handled from both sides. Maxie's fingers were already beneath her skirt and Charlotte was in the process of opening her blouse. All she had to do was lie there and enjoy it.

Something in the back of Sue Ellen's mind was repulsed by all this. Yet her body accepted the attention gladly. She knew, against her will, that it felt good. Charlotte had a loving touch, skilled in manipulating a woman's body so as to arouse the customer. And Maxie's little eyes appreciated her own cleanliness, the Italian silk blouse, the new crisp brassiere she wore beneath it.

Maybe I'll get pregnant, Sue Ellen repeated over and over. She clung to this thought as her body leaped into response to the four hands searching and probing.

She lay naked on the bed, watching Charlotte take off her own clothes now. Red lines from the girdle crisscrossed the pure white skin. The woman still had a pretty good figure except for the roll of fat hanging on the outside of her thighs. Her loosened stockings sagged to below the knees, giving the effect of a pair of boots. Then she crawled onto the bed beside Sue Ellen. She flopped one breast against Sue Ellen's mouth.

Instinctively the girl responded. She felt one of Maxie's hands slide under her buttocks and knew that the other was someplace on Charlotte.

"I love to see ladies loving each other," Maxie said. "Affection. Lots of affection. It makes the world go round."

"And then he gets in the middle," Charlotte whispered to Sue Ellen.

By now Sue Ellen was oblivious. All she knew was that her body lay surrounded by lots of warm, living flesh. She heard someone's breathing increase. Lips and legs and hands moved all over her. Reaching out she grabbed a thigh. By it's hairiness she knew it was Maxie's. He slithered in between the two women. Sue Ellen felt his smooth cheek against her own. The bed sagged. It creaked for awhile in time to the music. She reached up to embrace Maxie and her embrace included Charlotte.

"We make a sandwich," Maxie laughed.

I've got to get pregnant ... got to get pregnant.

The beer and the beans and Maxie and Charlotte all mixed together in a whirling despair that could find no end.

Unaware of the process of getting dressed again and leaving Jack's place, Sue Ellen got herself back home. She hadn't bothered to put on fresh make-up or tuck her blouse in neatly.

She managed to get the key in the lock. But the door opened by Richard's hand.

"My God," he said. "What's happened to you? I've been out of my mind."

"Why? What time is it?" Sue Ellen blubbered. Not waiting for an answer she staggered to the bedroom and fell asleep in her clothes.

The next morning Richard didn't go to work. He was sitting cross-legged in bed pulling on his upper lip when she finally awoke.

"Don't you think you owe me some explanation?" he said.

It took Sue Ellen a moment to get her bearings. She had difficulty recollecting why he looked so tense and strange.

When it came back to her, she turned away from him and drew the covers tight up to her chin. It made her feel like she was a child again, wrapped in a bunting. He didn't know about the doctor. He would hardly suspect about Charlotte and what's his name.

"Well?" Richard said.

"Do you love me?"

"Of course I love you. What's that got to do with anything? Do you know what you looked like when you came home? A regular ..." His discretion refused to permit the word to escape him.

Her mouth still tasted of beer. "If you love me, we'll just forget last night. It won't happen again, I promise you."

She heard his self-righteousness fizzle out. In its place came husbandly concern.

"I just want to know you aren't in any trouble."

"Rest assured."

She got out of bed and forced herself to make him breakfast. She didn't want Richard around the house. Confronted by his bewildered eyes, she could face neither him nor herself. After his third cup of coffee, she convinced him that it would be all right to go to the office.

Alone with herself, she drew a steaming bath and soaked in the tub. Would Richard have been so generous with his concern if he knew that she was barren?

CHAPTER SIXTEEN

"I went on a campaign to get myself pregnant. Really, I can't tell you all the horrible things I did in the next month. Every morning after Richard left the house, I went out. There were dozens of men, maybe hundreds. Big ones, little ones, young ones, not so young ones. It's all a blur. And the more men I slept with, the more I had to sleep with. Someone might have been standing over me with a whip, the way I felt driven."

"You hadn't heard from your father in all this time?"

"No, of course not." Sue Ellen's voice spat the words with resentment. "Why should I have? He didn't care about me. That fact was proven when I got married."

"And you still say that the reason you started going out was because you wanted to become impregnated?"

"I know you're getting at something, doctor. But I don't know what."

"Think a moment. You say the only person you ever loved was your father. And you say he rejected you, without any question of a doubt, at the time of your marriage. Also you have realized during the course of these conversations that you wanted to possess him."

"Say it, Dr. Ross. I wanted to go to bed with him."

"All right then, you've said it. Now, what do you make of the picture that you've drawn here?"

"Oh, no. You're not going to sit there and tell me I started on the merry-go-round because I was looking to find my father all over again."

"Didn't you say that you'd rather he had come to live with you than Richard?"

"Yes. But..."

"But what?" Dr. Ross was insistent. "Face yourself now, Sue Ellen. You've mentioned nightmares. And yet you've never once told me about any of them. They were about your father, weren't they? Did you perhaps see yourself murdering him in some fashion?"

"Yes. How did you know?"

"It's rather inevitable. You see, dreams are often a form of wish fulfillment. They are egocentric and primitive. In dreams we take no heed of social mores. All your life you have been trying to free yourself of this unsatisfying tie to your father. Yes, you loved him. But he did not return your subconscious demands. You felt neglected. Neglected by mother and father alike. But since you had to believe that your father returned your love, you were torn by conflicting emotions. On the one hand to possess him. On the other, to free yourself because it was impossible for you to possess him. The climax to these vague anxieties came at your wedding. And you are perfectly fertile. Remember, you took a physical before we started analysis. The reason you were unable to conceive was because it would take away your excuse to continue looking for your father."

"But what about the doctor's report to me?"

"I have checked with him. You had a tipped uterus. What he told you, Sue Ellen, was that you *had* been unable to become pregnant. By readjusting the position of your womb, you were once again capable."

His words, though spoken low, stabbed at her like pellets of sleet. Sue Ellen's arms, tense at her sides, clenched and unclenched. "No. I don't believe you. It's too impossible."

"Perhaps not now. But in time you will come to accept. But there is much you still have to work through."

"Then I have to tell you all about those horrors. What I did until the final thing that brought me to you."

"As you wish. But eventually, you will have to speak them out. The catharsis of talking, they call it. As we bring forth the demons plaguing us, we explain them. They become real and take on a life size. Imagination, in time, stops blowing them up."

"But you know what I did. You've handled cases like me before."

"I might know. But the question is, do you?"

"Oh, doctor. How can I forget!"

For six months she managed to keep her activities a secret from Richard. In order that dinner would be ready, she hired a cook. She drank and ate and slept and thought about nothing except the next man. The man who might give her a child.

Perversely her sexual relations with Richard diminished to nothing. It gave her a strange kind of pleasure when he would edge toward her at night and try to make love. Sometimes she would let him, afraid that he might become suspicious otherwise. And finally Richard's demands took the cycle of once every two weeks. This was quite tolerable to Sue Ellen. If her nerves had been in order, she might have continued this camouflage indefinitely.

But the phallic symbol now wielded full sway. She would awake during the night imagining that a male organ was lying beside her on the pillow. Or she would break out into a sweat during her dreams and come to in the convulsive throes of a psychic orgasm.

That was the worst. She found that she could sit in a chair and imagine herself having intercourse with such reality that her vaginal muscles contracted with utter conviction. The horror of this became a fascinating game. Sometimes she could not go out because Mrs. Bower was expected at the house and then she would sit with a copy of a magazine and induce orgasm after orgasm.

The nervous exertion began to pare weight from her frame. She didn't bother to examine herself, knowing that the mirror had no complimentary picture to reflect. She was eating less. All food tasted like cotton batting. Between her sleeplessness, her constant fear that Richard would discover all and her sensitive nerves, she found it less and less within her power to remain agreeable.

When Richard came home for dinner, she would pick on him for being five minutes late. She herself might have come in just a second before. But this made no difference. Then she would bicker with him for working too hard. In the next breath she objected to his not accepting the vice presidency.

And Richard would bring her flowers. He suggested that they take a cruise to Bermuda. She could see the sincere worry on his face but she felt powerless to respond.

Finally Richard insisted that they take a vacation. If she didn't need one, he certainly did.

"If we have just a week someplace together, everything'll straighten out," he said softly. "I know it will."

"Everything would be fine if your mother would stop trying to mind my business," she snapped, pushing away her plate of soup.

"I'm sure Mother isn't important enough to take away your appetite."

"She is. I can't stand her anymore."

Sue Ellen disregarded the hurt look which made Richard drop his glance to the plate.

"Sometimes I think I'm married to a whole family instead of just one man."

Her tantrums availed nothing. Sue Ellen found herself imprisoned on a ship with Richard. There was little she could do without him finding out. Wherever she went, if she took a stroll on the deck, there was Richard.

They swam together in the pool, played table tennis. His body was beginning to turn a lovely copper shade but it didn't impress Sue Ellen.

Obsessed by the thought of shaking him off, she could find privacy only in the bathroom. Richard insisted that she get some sleeping pills from the ship's doctor.

"I don't need pills," she yelled at him from behind the bathroom door. "What I need is a real vacation. A vacation from you!"

When she came out, Richard had left the cabin. At first she thought that he was probably lurking outside. For something to do meanwhile, she picked up an atomizer and sprayed a mist of verbena over her hair. Her fury of words had been stopped too shortly. She almost wished he would return so she could relieve herself of them. Half an hour went by. She paced the cabin, changed from shorts into slacks. But Richard didn't come back. She went outside and glanced about on the deck. Two children were bouncing a rubber ball and some older couples lay reading magazines or jotting post cards.

Sue Ellen felt a touch of triumph. She sauntered down to some boys playing shuffle board and watched their lithe muscles glittering in the sunlight.

When she got back to the cabin, Richard was dressing for dinner. He didn't even glance at her. She took out her evening dress. The silence between them lasted until bedtime.

In a voice straining to be civil, Richard said, "If there's something wrong between us, I think we ought to discuss it."

She didn't hear the pain or the sadness. Focused on herself, Sue Ellen could only understand that he was being cold, almost brutal. He didn't love her anymore. He wanted her to ask for a divorce so he would be free to find a woman who could bear children.

"I've been trying," she said in a tone equally civil. "I've been trying very hard. But I don't think we have enough in common. We're different. Too different. What's the use of dragging it out any longer?" She found her aloof manner very satisfactory.

"I didn't know," he answered in a voice hardly audible.

She knew Richard wasn't a fighter. Just a matter of time. She would have her separation. Smiling to herself in the dark, Sue Ellen slept almost well that night.

They dragged out the rest of their trip like two strangers forced into each other's company by outside circumstances.

When they arrived back in New York, Sue Ellen already imagined herself divorced. This expectancy blinded her to any attempt at reconciliation. Richard's overtures went unnoticed. She had thoroughly convinced herself that he wanted a divorce.

And so once again the world had proved to her that loneliness and isolation were the true realities. No longer could she depend on the security of marriage. It was a mirage.

She began to go out during the day, seeking not pregnancy this time, but oblivion. With a strange man's arms around her, the hideous thoughts evaporated and for that instant she could feel something closer to love, to stability. It made no difference who the lover was. Sex had become an addiction—the more she fed it, the more she craved. She sought only to annihilate her mind through the processes of the body.

No longer was it necessary to keep up a front for Richard's sake. She would go out in the morning and wander through the park or along Seventh Avenue, searching for the answer of eagerness in a stranger's eyes. She became familiar with hotels where she could stay through the night.

The drifters who picked her up took Sue Ellen to drab rooms where plaster would drop onto her face as she lay squirming on the mattress. Or sometimes it might be a rich man who owned his own home in New Jersey. She would stand naked at the window and look across at the city's skyline, misted in smoke. It was all the same to her, rich man or poor.

When she would finally return to her own apartment, her swollen eyelids told the mute but sordid story of her adventures.

Richard began staying away from home now too. When, sometimes, they would meet there accidentally, he tried not to look at her. But Sue Ellen's conscience goaded her into fights with him. She needed to hear the nasty words which would make the nightmare of her life tangible.

"Go on," she yelled at him, "say something. Call me a bum. I know that's what you're thinking." Her voice was shrill.

"I don't know what to call you," he said. "But I think you should see a doctor, Sue Ellen. You need help."

The truth of it jabbed her. "*I* need help? What about you? You and your prissy ways. Mamma's boy. Mamma still feeding you supper. Mamma still making sure her little sonny boy gets to bed on time."

Actually Mrs. Bower had begun stopping by to see that the maid had everything attended to. Signs of Mrs. Bower's presence accused Sue Ellen when she came home after two or three days' absence.

"Someone has to look after this place."

"Then go and marry your mother. I'm leaving."

She ran into the bedroom and slammed the door shut so hard that a picture on the wall slipped sideways. She flung open drawers and began throwing her clothes on the bed.

Richard came in. "No need to do that," he said softly. "You can stay. I'll go."

"Then go. Get the hell out. Who needs you!"

In less than fifteen minutes, Richard had an overnight case filled with some shirts and various toiletries.

"If you need me," he said, buttoning his coat, "if you need anything …"

Sue Ellen threw an ashtray at him.

She heard the outside door shut. And now she was alone in the big apartment. Silence clung to the walls. Mirrors reflected furniture and more silence. She ran through the rooms, turning on radios. Each blared a different station.

"What do I care?" she yelled at the empty apartment, thrusting her arms ceilingward. "I'm free ... free ..."

In a few minutes she dialed half a dozen of the phone numbers collected from men who were anxious to see her again. Five of them said, yes, they would be right over. Then Sue Ellen made sure the front door was standing ajar. Whoever wanted to come in was welcome. She kicked off her shoes, tore and pulled her stockings off. Then she dragged down her girdle and panties and flung them away.

The men began to arrive, curious and anxious to experience Sue Ellen's hospitality again. One looked furtively at the other, wondering what was going on. Sue Ellen opened bottles of Scotch as she danced about with nothing on but her dress. Through it one could see the firm outline of her breasts. She had lost more than thirty pounds in the past few months and the dress hung limply around her shoulders and thinned hips.

"It's a party, boys." She laughed a raucous, anguished sound. "It's a great big get together."

One of the better dressed men had presence of mind enough to go lock the door.

Sue Ellen took long gulps from the whiskey. Then she lifted her dress high above her belly and began to dance a furious mambo. Her smile touched each leering face but her eyes saw nothing except a skeleton of death, dancing close to greet her. She lay down on the living room floor and draped the hem of her skirt over her face.

"Damn it," she screamed. "Somebody .... me."

She felt a rush of blood to her stomach. Then everything went black.

When she came to, it wasn't in the apartment. Sue Ellen looked groggily around. Slowly a white metal bedpost came into focus. White walls. A white sheet covered her.

"What's happening?" she said, meaning the words to be loud. Her voice came out in little more than a whisper. She moved her head and saw a bell sitting on the white night table near the pillow. With effort she lifted her hand and let one finger fall on the button. The tiny clapper made a sound that echoed through the chambers of her head.

In a few minutes a very young girl came in. A starched white cap perched on her soft hair. She bent over and took Sue Ellen's wrist in her warm fingers.

"Why ... am I ..." Sue Ellen finished her sentence with a mute question, searching the coffee brown eyes.

"You've had a little break down," the girl offered. "It will be best for you to rest here a few days. Your husband is waiting outside. I'll get him for you." Her voice was like rippling water.

"No," Sue Ellen said.

She recalled her last waking moment. She couldn't possibly face Richard. Not yet. A great ocean of drowsiness ebbed and flowed in her. She wanted to sleep and sleep and sleep. Her eyelids fluttered. The young nurse went out of focus again.

The next time she awakened a doctor stood at the foot of her bed, reading a chart attached to the metal pole.

"Good morning," he said cheerily. "I'm Dr. Whiting. How do you feel today?"

A stabbing sensation went through her leg. She felt a bandage on her thigh. "How should I feel?" She didn't like his smiling face and she didn't like the antiseptic smell coming at her from all sides.

"Much better, I hope," he said, ignoring her ill humor. He came around and pulled a chair up beside the bed. She watched him place a stethescope in his ears. "You've been suffering, among other things, from malnutrition," he said. "Your leg might hurt a bit from the intravenous feedings."

She let him put the cold metal against her chest.

"You'll need a little attention here before you're ready to leave. The nurse will take you out on the grounds in a day or so. It's really quite lovely here."

"I'm sure I'll enjoy myself," she said nastily.

"We hope so."

For the next week she absolutely refused to see Richard or anyone else who tried to visit. Trays of the plain hospital food were rejected. But the less she ate, the more she had to submit to the needle. After a few such experiences, she decided that mouth feeding was the lesser evil.

And slowly she began to enjoy the nurses who were always there when she wanted someone to talk to. No matter what hour of the night, she could press the bell and someone would come keep her company.

CHAPTER SEVENTEEN

"That attention meant more to me than all the medical care science had to offer. You know, doctor, I've spent my life looking for someone to take care of me. And that hospital was the best crutch I ever found."

"Not your salvation?"

"No. Of course not. I used to think that if my father had kept me or come to New York, or if this had happened or that, I would be all right now. The foundations I built in my head were all wrong. So nothing could have saved me, except to reconstruct the whole mental house."

"You're really making progress."

"Do you think so?"

"Yes, definitely. The moment you stopped blaming other people, you started on the road to better mental health."

"Oh, I know I have to take on the responsibility of myself. I often had a glimmering of this but it managed to slip away before I could pin it down. This means, I guess, that I never really wanted to. It's hard to give up the old ways. Old habits are always easier. And I certainly surrounded myself with old habits when I was in the sanitarium."

Sue Ellen began to put on weight again. She had always been three or four pounds on the voluptuous side. Looking at herself regaining the old curves gave her new confidence. Her eyes didn't look so wild anymore, either. The nurses were kind, Dr. Whiting impervious to her criticisms. Altogether she had to admit, though privately, that it was very satisfying in the hospital. Best of all, they gave her something to make her sleep at night. This relief from morbid dreams worked miracles. She decided to be kind and see Richard.

They strolled under the hospital's shade trees and Sue Ellen told him about the good care she was getting.

"You're looking wonderful," he said.

She waited for him to mention something about their divorce. "I guess this is the vacation I needed," she said. Her calm felt so secure, so all encompassing that she decided to tell him something. "I owe you an explanation. About our children. The children we don't have."

Richard took out a little cigar and lit it. He looked like an imitation Martin. He was born to be successful. Every inch of him was a solid businessman.

"I think you ought to know that I'm barren." She said the words simply and without excuse.

Calmly he brought the match flame to the cigar and inhaled. "I've known that for a long time," he said. "But I was waiting for you to tell me. I wasn't all that confident, my dear. I wanted you to prove that you trusted me."

Someplace high in a tree a bird chirrupped and Sue Ellen looked toward the notes because she could not face Richard.

"Well," she said helplessly, "I guess that's that."

"Adoption agencies are for people like us, you know."

The words stung. They made her feel somehow underprivileged. "Would you want an adopted child?"

"Why not?"

He was always so sensible, so damned sensible. Little did he understand the torture she had gone through since the day she had found out. And here stood Richard, implying that none of this made any difference. How could men be so callous, so selfish?

"I guess I'll have to think about it," she said.

After he left, she thought about it very hard indeed. But the more she thought, the more she hated Richard for not having saved her all this agony. Trust him. Have confidence in him. Always, it was the sneaky, underhanded one who wanted people to trust. If anything, their conversation had proved to her how right it was that she should get a divorce.

The longer she stayed in the hospital, the stronger she felt. She thought about getting a job and staying on, helping others to regain themselves as she had. Eight weeks now and she hadn't been overly plagued by a need for sex. When the urge came upon her, she would simply cross her legs and soon it would die its natural death with a ghost of a climax. It gave her confidence to know that the slightest movement or pressure against her genitals was enough to hold her until the next time.

When Martin came to visit her, she could truthfully say that she didn't miss a thing from the outside world. She hadn't realized how completely Martin had sunk into old age until he came to see her. Sue Ellen's growing vitality emphasized Martin's decline. His muscular development was rapidly turning into softness. The spring of his life had run out like an old clock. He seemed to be waiting and counting the days until his heart stopped ticking.

She felt sorry for Martin, but what could she do to help?

"I'm fine," Martin said. "You're in the hospital, not me. I go to the club every week. Once in a while Jeff honors me by going to a hockey game. I don't know what's the matter with that boy." His eyes were thoughtful.

She could have told him what was the matter with Jeff. But Sue Ellen had hopes that a girl would get hold of him yet. They talked about Jeff because it was easier than speaking about either one of them.

And when she saw Martin to the door, she felt glad for the few years she had given him. No doubt the ghost of her mother haunted the man. Being neither dead nor alive, she held Martin in the same state of suspended animation.

From her vantage point safe in the country, Sue Ellen could look back over all the people she had known and understand that none of them were what she really wanted. It was good to be a doctor, a nurse and help people. Everyone needed some kind of help. The most honest could sympathize with this human need and devote themselves to filling it. That was one way to beat loneliness. At twenty odd she was not too old to start a career along those lines. She might not have the concentration to become a nurse, but she could be a nurse's aid. This humble beginning would satisfy her. Give her something to hold onto. And perhaps in time, she would gain the strength to go to school.

These thoughts were like warm blankets at night and Sue Ellen clung to them, believing that God had suddenly blessed her with a rebirth. She read through some text books in the hospital library and they fed her with ambition.

Just as the vision of her splendid new future was beginning to jell, Dr. Whiting announced that she was well enough to be dismissed.

"You're in top physical condition," he said. "You don't have to stay around here with the sick ones anymore. Go out and live. But do it sensibly."

She looked at him, leaning back in the swivel chair behind his desk. "I don't want to leave," she blurted. "I want to stay here and help."

The words surprised him but he recovered his equanimity in a second. "There's nothing to stop you from helping," he said. "But I'm sure a beautiful girl like you doesn't want to stay in a hospital room."

He wasn't understanding.

"Maybe I'm not as well as you think." She searched desperately for some convincing argument. "Maybe I'll have a relapse." She could see herself out in the world. No one to talk to at night. Surrounded by the miseries of people who didn't know they were suffering.

"I'd better stay another week or so. Make sure. After all," she said defensively. "My husband's paying for it. I'm entitled."

And so she stayed for another week. But in her heart, Sue Ellen knew that she was taking up space and service without cause. Clinging to her ambition to join the medical staff, she bolstered her courage and packed her few clothes.

Richard met her and they rode home. She stepped inside the apartment and its peculiar, familiar smell recalled all the tatters of her life. Her temples began to ache.

"I'd better lie down," she said and went to her bedroom. Forcing her eyes shut, she tried to recapture all the good intentions which had filled her life these past three months. She must sign up for school immediately. Books, homework, studying. These would keep her going. Her body began to sweat as though she stood in a dark alley and a cold gun poked her ribs.

When Richard came to bed, she flung herself against his chest and encircled him with her arms. Though her head was feverish, her toes felt cold.

"You won't leave me," she said. "Promise you'll never leave me. I'll be good to you, darling. I'll do anything you say. Just don't leave me."

She heard him sigh. His fingers stroked her neck soothingly. "It wasn't I who wanted to leave you," he said.

"Well, I was stupid and foolish. That's how people get sometimes. But you know I love you. You know that, don't you, Richard?"

"Yes. I know."

She needed him to prove this and only one way could convince her. Unconsciously her hands sought beneath Richard's pajamas. "All I want to do is make you happy. Why don't you want me, Richard? Why don't you?"

Insensibly she was crying. The bitter taste of despair flooded her. Nothing that Richard said could make her believe that she was safe, that he wouldn't leave her in the morning. She made him take her again and again. Yet each time it felt like a lie. Something kept telling Sue Ellen that his mind was elsewhere. On another woman, perhaps.

"Honestly," he said after an hour. "I think you need psychiatric help. How can you ask if there's been another woman in my life? Do I have time to think about anything else but you? My work has slipped. I've cost the company thousands of dollars worth of mistakes because my mind had been preoccupied. For both of us, Sue Ellen, I beg you. Go to a psychiatrist. Heaven knows where you'll wind up otherwise."

What Richard said was true. Yet his words filled her with cold terror. She could imagine a psychiatrist delving through her past, bringing to light all the dirty episodes which had filled it. No one must know what she had done with her years. A rich girl, with all the advantages of home and family. Her behavior had been inexcusable.

But still, because she had to have Richard love her, Sue Ellen agreed. "You find a doctor and I'll go to him."

"That's the only sensible thing to do," he said.

Together they lay awake for the rest of the night, each thinking his own futile thoughts. Sue Ellen felt the dimensions of her body and tried to imagine that the head which directed it was insane. Movies of people sitting unkempt and lethargic recalled themselves to her. Shock treatments. Two metal wires attached to her temples and electricity shooting back and forth between them. Mother . . . .

Then she began to think it would be all right if she simply behaved herself. Plans for school were sensible. If she enrolled right away and Richard saw that she was attending to her studies, he would forget all this psychiatrist business. She resolved to go immediately in the morning. And she decided not to tell Richard, but let him see for himself.

She could hardly wait until after breakfast. Then she put on a sober looking skirt and jacket. Not too much lipstick. No earrings. The completed picture looked very businesslike, very medical. She rode down to the Bellevue Nursing School, making sure not to smoke so that the registration officer wouldn't smell nicotine on her fingers.

Sue Ellen, accustomed to having things her own way, could hardly believe that she would have to wait until the following semester before classes started. She offered more money. She begged that they allow her to sit in and take notes even without credit.

Nothing availed her. She lost her temper and language poured out of her mouth which was hardly ladylike. Suddenly realizing the appearance she made, Sue Ellen turned and fled from the building.

All she could see now was a nut house and herself barred in. There was no hope. If Richard thought she was crazy, how would anyone else believe otherwise?

She didn't want to go home now. And she certainly didn't want to face Richard. A policeman's horse stood across the street relieving itself. She watched fascinated. And the old path to forgetfulness beckoned her.

The Village was a place Sue Ellen had come to know well. On its crooked streets or in its bars she could always find someone who needed what she was after. Occasionally the man she had picked up turned out to be a woman dressed in men's clothing. But this didn't make any difference. Whoever, whatever these people were, they could give to her, demanding nothing of promises for tomorrow. Faces floated by, like buoys on a misted ocean, each a moment of saving light which would be bypassed in the morning.

Sue Ellen had an affection for this part of town because no one forced themselves to be respectable. People were what they were. And nobody but tourists called anyone else names.

She rode as far as Washington Square Arch and walked into the park. A spark of confidence comforted her. There was sure to be somebody any moment who would respond to what she had in her heart. She sat down on a bench and listened to kids playing with each other behind her in the grass. Sandalled women sat rocking baby carriages. One squeezed a bit of milk from her breast and then put her nipple into the infant's mouth. Nobody stopped to stare. No one gave a damn. The Good Humor man stood beside his yellow truck, handing cups and I-Stix to a group of N.Y.U. students who had just gotten out of class. Sue Ellen looked at their notebooks and wondered if she would ever, ever have the right combination of circumstances in her life.

It was hard to remain motionless on the wooden bench. The nervous center had already begun its insistent pulsing. She licked her lips and glanced around to make sure she didn't miss anyone who might be attractive. Attractive, of course, meant available, but she would have liked to keep up a certain deception for the sake of her conscience.

Two girls sat down beside her, both dressed in sneakers and trousers and lumber jackets. Though their clothing was exactly alike, the bodies that filled them could not have been more different. The tightness of their slacks made the short one shorter and rounder, the tall one taller and thinner. They could have been two college kids except for the faces. Each had a fringe of greying bangs which highlighted the dark smudges under the eyes. The round one also had a smudge of dark hair on her upper lip, giving her face an unwashed appearance.

It was the round one who leaned across to Sue Ellen. "Hey," she said, "don't I remember you from someplace?"

This wasn't a line. A sincere innocence looked out at Sue Ellen from the hazel eyes.

Maybe they had met. Perhaps at some point, when she wasn't too sober, they had danced or taken a drink together. If it had been anything more intimate, the round one would have remembered.

Sue Ellen said, "I'm sure we have." She looked back at the tall one, who scrutinized her over the round one's head. "Anyway, I'm looking for a place to stay. Maybe you can help me?"

Until this moment it had not occurred to Sue Ellen that she was going to leave Richard forever.

The round one turned to the tall one. "Corky, you know any place?"

Corky looked at Sue Ellen's alligator shoes. They were plain pumps, but obviously well-made. "I don't think I know of any place for free."

"I didn't mean that," Sue Ellen put in.

Corky said, "If you're willin' to pay eighty dollars a month, there's a nice basement apartment on Jane Street a boy I know wants to sublet."

The round one, named Elva, was all for showing it to Sue Ellen right away. Her anxiousness to please didn't have any sexual implication, Sue Ellen knew. Each of the girls wore a plain wedding band on her right pinky. Apparently Elva was satisfied. But with Corky, there were possibilities.

The three of them went down Waverly Place, descended stairs to a black painted door. Corky lifted a brass knocker and let it fall. Someone called, "Just a moment," in a high fluttery voice.

When the door opened a blonde curly headed boy stood holding the collar of a boxer. "Hurry in," he said, "before Abraham gets away from me."

Sue Ellen went first and the two women followed in a kind of deference to her femininity.

"The lady here is thinking to take your place," Corky said.

"Oh, just in time. I have to be out of here tomorrow and I'm just at my wit's end about what to do with Abraham. Mother detests animals of all shapes and sizes."

For a moment Sue Ellen thought of Terry, living now with Martin and Jeff.

The apartment had scarlet drapes and cushions scattered about the floor. Its Japanese style table lent a clean, economical elegance reminiscent of ads in decorating magazines for young moderns.

"It's lovely here," Sue Ellen said.

The two girls were sitting on the floor, tossing a ball between them for Abraham to catch. It had a bell inside which jingled softly.

"Oh, it's nothing yet," the boy said. "I'm waiting for next season and a few new Johns. Stingy people are such a bore."

Corky said, "I told her it would be eighty dollars a month."

"Well, for you, honey, I can make it seventy five."

Sue Ellen took out her wallet and gave him a hundred and fifty. "I didn't know about the dog," she said. "But it's all right, if I can stay here tonight, that is."

"There's plenty of room," he said. "I'll show you around."

She didn't really care but the boy was so proud of his place that he couldn't deny him the pleasure. Duly she admired the potted vines growing down from brass bowls high on the bedroom wall. From the barred windows she could see the feet of strollers, but they couldn't see in. The cafe curtains in both rooms would give her as much privacy as she needed.

They came back to the living room and Sue Ellen said to the girls, "I want to thank you both."

"We'll be seeing you," Corky said.

It was a strangely light feeling to have a place where Richard wouldn't be able to find her. She decided to phone him so he wouldn't have the police chasing around the city for her. Instead of waiting until he got home, she called Richard at the office, where he wouldn't be able to argue with her or try to talk her out of this decision. The impatience in her voice was so obvious that Richard hardly said a word.

So now she was free. Free to find love. Free to seek out others like herself who were sliding fast to a destiny they dared not imagine.

The boy left early the next morning after spending half the night in various bars. Sue Ellen listened as he dressed and chatted and gave her final instructions about Abraham. She liked the idea of having a dog again. It was a good excuse for roaming the streets without appearing to be a loiterer.

She took Abraham with her to the stores and bought a whole new wardrobe of Village style clothes. As she buttoned the tight corduroy pants and belted the suede jacket, all recollection of being Mrs. Bower Jr. disappeared. She took her wedding ring off and slipped it into her purse.

CHAPTER EIGHTEEN

"The rest is self-evident. You can imagine what I did for the next five years."

Dr. Ross put down the note book. She heard him fold his glasses and lay them on the desk blotter.

"I know," she said. "You're going to say that I have to talk it out. The whole business is so offensive to me. I don't think I have the courage. Maybe I'm afraid, still. Anyway, I'm here. I haven't missed a single session. That must count for something. How difficult it was to make that final decision for analysis. If I had listened to Richard, perhaps I would have been well by now."

"But Richard did not finally prompt you?"

"No. He got a divorce. I get my alimony every month. We never see each other. There's nothing. There's no one in my life who matters...."

For two months Sue Ellen was on a Lesbian kick. Not that it made any difference whether she kissed a man or a woman. But Corky would come around at night and they would go out to bars that catered to women. It was so easy to stand behind the juke box with a glass of beer and know that one of the ape-like creatures at the bar would soon come sidling over to her. And women were considerate. They took special pains to do the thing properly. And the more she wanted, the more they were willing to give. It made them feel masculine.

Yet, inevitably, they would go away and she'd be left with the sound of her own breathing and Abraham's light snore drifting up to her from his wicker bed.

Sometimes it would rain and she would think it better not to take him out in the wet. And she'd throw the bell-ball and Abraham would run and bring it back to her, standing straight up with one paw on each of her knees. He stared at her with the quizzical series of creases very deep in his forehead. She'd touch his slanted ears and talk to him as though he were human.

There was nobody and nothing to run away from now. Sue Ellen wondered why the restlessness, why the uneasy feeling of impending disaster. And then she took Abraham out in the rain anyway and walked and walked. And sometimes came home alone. But Abraham had been trained not to sleep on the bed and he jumped off when she placed him beside her. Sue Ellen would turn the light on and watch Abraham's eyes wink and look at her and finally drift off into sleep.

But there were other nights too. With half a dozen people who were glad to eat the food she supplied and drink the beer. She could tire all of them and still be ready for another bout of love.

"How about the dog?" someone said one night. "Doesn't he get jealous?"

Abraham was sitting with a potato chip between his paws licking off the salt.

"Yeah, Susie girl. Why don't you give little Aby his turn?"

Perhaps the words were said in jest, perhaps they were serious. But they caused Sue Ellen to lose her temper. She kicked them all out of the apartment. Then she took away the potato chip and put her arms around Abraham's neck and cried into his ear that it was all right.

She went to sleep and dreamed that Abraham was wearing a plaid flannel shirt and lived in a woodsman's house. Though Abraham was still a dog in her dream, he walked on his hind legs and she could see, among other things, the undeveloped nipples on his belly. When she woke up, Sue Ellen had the pillow between her legs and it was all rumpled.

Consciously she had no desire to touch the dog. The dream appalled her more than anything she had ever done in her waking life. Its implications were clear and strangely enticing in a curious way. She tried not to think about it. The more she tried, the more she found herself wanting to stroke the dog. Devilishly Abraham was innocently very willing to accept Sue Ellen's attentions. He stood very still, apparently enjoying himself. Then he leaped up and tried to rub against her leg.

Sue Ellen ran into the bathroom and locked the door. She kept herself locked in until she was sure that she could remember the difference between animals and humans. She looked at herself in the mirror and laughed wildly. Were there any lengths to which she would not go? What kind of twisted brain was it her misfortune to possess? There must be a God. And if there were no such, then there must be a law for living. Where did she fit in? What was she? Who was she? Could nothing ever satisfy her? Was she doomed to burrow so deeply into sex that it would finally kill her?

Gladly she gave the boy back his apartment and the care of Abraham. But she would not go back uptown. She could not face any of her old ties. Even Martin was beyond her now. The only person with whom she would not be ashamed was her mother.

It was a sweetly acid thought. One which gave Sue Ellen a strange delight. Of all people, her mother would understand. Oversexed herself, mad enough to be hospitalized. Her mother would know all about Sue Ellen. And visiting her, she could learn what to expect as her own eventual fate.

For a few weeks Sue Ellen played with the idea. While she thought about it, she got herself another apartment. It was a nice place. Very respectable looking with a fireplace and a bedroom overlooking a back garden.

Though she had nothing to do with Richard except for the alimony checks, Sue Ellen used his name and its reputation as security in signing the lease. For a few days she went furniture shopping. It took her mind off the immediate problem of self and allowed her to mull over the advisability of going to visit her mother.

The seasons came and went. Every once in awhile, the thought of her mother returned, each time a little stronger, a little more convincing. She had begun to lose weight again. And as Sue Ellen pulled in her clothes, she remembered the sweet sixteen party, the bones showing on her mother's chest, the make-up smeared by a wild hand.

At last she could no longer avoid the pull to go to Long Island for that visit.

The train ride took almost two hours. With each station stop, she felt an increasing flush of hot and cold. She had no idea of what might confront her. It had been almost nine years. At one station she almost got off the train, but something held and she gripped the arm of the seat, her knuckles going white from the tension. People all around her sat peaceably reading magazines, chewing gum or just staring up at the ads. Would she ever know such peace for herself? She seemed to inhabit another world made up in shades of grey or livid red. Nothing in her mind had ever been as bright and crisp as this other world, so close, but beyond her touch.

She got off the train and waited for the local bus to take her out. Too nervous for driving, Sue Ellen had never owned a car. She put coins into the fare slot, heard the ping, ping-ping and took a seat behind the driver. The broad expanse of his back hid the view of the road. But she was looking down at the corrugated rubber matting in the aisle, unable to lift her head and face the looming blow of seeing her mother.

The sanitarium spread before her like a city. Composed of many buildings, it sprawled beneath the cloudless sky. Red brick, neatly mortared to hold its captured ghosts. It came to Sue Ellen with a painful jolt how many people there must be locked away in these buildings. What was it? One out of seven in every home would provide an emotionally disturbed person needing mental help. And the average was rising every year.

Elsewhere in the city, people were home now from Sunday church, eager for dinner and the week end papers. Or was this a myth? She had never known the kind of general American living which you could see in the movies any day of the week.

Her heels sent bits of gravel scampering as she walked to the visitors' entrance. Others converged there with her and some exchanged a smile of greeting with her. This was the one place in the world where none could play the snob. Each knew the reason for the other's presence. Each had been brought to the same low and none could pretend otherwise.

Inside she waited on line for her visiting pass. An attendant directed her up the stairs. She passed windows, so many windows with a wired view of the outside.

And then she was in a large room where people sat talking to people and it was difficult to tell who of each group would get up to leave when the hours were over. Her only clue to this lay in the givers of brown paper bags. Those who munched fruit, those who untied paper boxes and bit into doughnuts. They were the unchosen.

Sue Ellen held fast to these contemplations as she waited. Then she saw a hefty attendant approaching her. Behind the attendant was a little woman with mouse colored hair tied in a single braid. This hair which had once been so blonde, so fluffy was not even an honest grey. It seemed not to have faded but rather to have forgotten its own color, just as the eyes and the nose and the mouth seemed not to remember that they must make a single face. Horribly, each feature possessed its own expression. The total effect was that of a wooden figure that had been made by a bad carpenter. She was led by the attendant and seated on a chair by Sue Ellen.

"This is your daughter, sweetie," the attendant said, one hand in the pocket of her apron. "Your daughter Sue Ellen. You remember her." Then she nodded to Sue Ellen and drifted away.

"Hello, Mother."

She knew she was supposed to reach over and kiss her mother but her neck remained stiff on her shoulders. A crazy fear gripped her that this thing which possessed her mother was contagious.

The woman's mouth twitched in a series of jerking smiles. No words came from her lips.

A conversation behind them interrupted with its bickering about whether Irving or Morris should fill in the income tax form.

"How are you?" Sue Ellen persisted. It was hardly the question to ask. But she could think of nothing else. Her eyes feasted on the prospect of finding herself in the appearance of her mother. Would her own lips gather dry pieces of skin like this? Would blue veins come out on her forehead, sallow from the years of being inactive?

"You're a big girl. My daughter." The words sounded rusty.

"Yes, I'm a big girl. I'm twenty-five now, Mother. Almost twenty-six. I think about you often." And this was no lie.

Her mother's throat moved as though she were trying to speak. But she had to swallow a few times and her fingers kept playing with a worn handkerchief crumpled into a sweaty ball.

"You think about me?" It was part question, part statement.

"Oh yes. Someday we'll go shopping together, the way we used to. Would you like that?"

How long ago had it been since they had gone anywhere together? Sue Ellen herself could hardly remember. Why should she expect her mother to?

"Toy soldiers." The eyes flickered away to the barred windows.

For a moment the words made no sense. Then incredibly Sue Ellen remembered that Martin had been a soldier. Was she thinking of Martin, then? All these years with nothing but the thought that she had married Martin too late?

"Would you like me to bring you some toy soldiers? The next time I come?"

The next time. Would there be a next? Had she the strength to go through another visit? And if so, to what avail? It could be that her mother did not want to see her even this time. She could be a symbol of the wrong wedding, the wrong life. Imposing herself like this. A selfish act. Her own hands were playing with the snap of her purse. Anxious, unnerved. She could almost feel her own cheekbones pushing tautly at her skin, the way her mother's did.

The torture went on. Comparing feature for feature, Sue Ellen knew that indeed she was her mother's child.

Somewhere a bell rang through the halls. The round clock, high on a far wall, noted the hour. Sue Ellen gathered her courage and reached across, brushing her lips against her mother's forehead. It felt hot and dried out.

"Stay well," Sue Ellen murmured.

The attendant returned and helped her mother to stand. "I'm glad to see you." Her mind found a last word. "Daughter."

She sat there watching until the attendant and her mother had disappeared into one of the many rooms beyond.

Sue Ellen didn't have the composure for the long train ride home. She was trembling and feverish and dragged down by a weight of sadness. She could imagine all the years her mother had struggled against this final fate.

And how soon would it be before this same end came for herself? The bus took her back to the train but she went into a local bar and dropped quarters into the juke box. The loud music made no headway against the drift of her thoughts. She logged her brain with beer and more beer, waiting for her body to take over, waiting for the inevitable thirst of her nerves for another person who could blot out the future.

Perversely the more she drank, the clearer her mind became. It felt knife sharp. It focused on great distances of sprawling humanity devoured by the thrust and pull of her aching loins. It sucked in men and women by the thousands without names, without faces.

She pushed a ten dollar bill onto the counter and went out into the windy darkness. Private houses allowed her to see above them to the millions of stars ageless and clear in the curving universe. Millions of people infesting this tiny spinning ball of earth and none enough to quench the violent searching demon that was herself. She lunged across to the train station, staggered down the stairs and into a waiting car. The yellow glaring lights made her blink. She didn't belong here. She belonged back there. With her mother. One hand reached up. It wanted to tear away the clothes and show these placid humans that she was not one of them. She wanted to stand naked and have them see that she was ... a mad creature who must be burned and destroyed.

But much as she wanted to do this, she managed in one last muster of strength to control herself. She found a seat in the corner and folded her arms across her chest. Rigid in this position, she sat all the way home.

Safe in the apartment, she put on a long playing record and continued to drink until insensibility claimed her.

She slept until late afternoon of the next day. And when she awoke, she tried to go back to sleep, not willing to face the day. Not willing to face herself. But she was awake nevertheless. Her mouth, dry and swollen, reminded her of the cracked lips she had seen. Her hair needed a washing. It looked dull. It looked lost. Her head throbbed. She needed a Bromo but the medicine cabinet was empty. Yet she couldn't go out on the street. She dared not go out, afraid of what she might do. Afraid that one uncontrolled act would take her from the civilized world and remove her to that other, murky place.

For days she paced the apartment, alternately drinking and sleeping. And one day she came to. She did not know which day of the week it was, but it was a day blessed by heaven. Sue Ellen lay on the unmade bed, stared sightlessly at the ceiling and knew that she had no alternative. If she did not seek help now, she might never be able to get help again.

Weakly, with trembling fingers, she picked up the phone and called Richard.

CHAPTER NINETEEN

"And that's how I got here. All the bad things Mother did to me throughout my life culminated in this final good one. I don't hate her. How can I? Believe me, I know what she must have gone through. The problems Jeff or Martin or Richard have are nothing in comparison with my poor mother. I'm so sorry for her. How she managed to control herself all those years, I don't know. But I can imagine the thoughts that went through her mind, the dirty words, the bawdy songs, the desire to tear off her clothes and run naked in the streets. She had more control than I did, that's certain. Perhaps if she had less control, she would have understood that she needed help. Speaking of control, it's coming back to me, a little at a time. I don't understand why. Sometimes I can go for days. Then I slip. But the normal feeling always returns. I've learned to expect it."

"As you learn to live with your past, the symptom gradually diminishes. What, after all, is a symptom but the representation of some painful experience forced out of consciousness? That's why it is so difficult to uproot. In a very real sense, the symptom is an emotional outlet. That's why patients are loathe to give it up. One might say it represents a morbid gain. As a normal, wholesome outlet is substituted, the symptom is yielded."

"Yes, I understand part of what you say. I guess one's sex life is a symptom by itself. If it's healthy, the person stands a greater chance of being healthy."

"Exactly. Abnormal sex seems to obstruct normal functioning in other spheres. The process is retroactive. The more you can relate to others and yourself in a real sense, the better your sex life. And the better your sex life ..."

"The more it reflects the rest of me." Sue Ellen stretched and turned to look out the window. "Remember, Doctor, I said there was nobody and nothing in my life that mattered?"

"Yes, I remember."

"Well, that's beginning to change. I do have somebody. I have myself. And I'm going to work at this career of myself until it's worthy and can attract the kind of people who are worthwhile in return." She looked at her watch and saw that another session was coming to a close. "You know, Doctor, sometimes it's very pleasant to be in this office."

Sue Ellen got up from the couch, smiling with the appreciation she could never completely put into words, yet knowing that Dr. Ross understood her. She watched him fold his glasses and lay them on the blotter with the familiar gentleness she had come to trust. For a moment Sue Ellen wondered what he must be like as a human being outside of this office. Then the thought flashed away and she moved toward the door. She was content with the feeling of life's richness and promise for her.

In the waiting room she paused to smooth kidskin gloves over her fingers, recalling how different it had been that first day when she had dashed in, wild and frightened. The nurse, seated behind her desk, was speaking now on the phone and Sue Ellen listened to her voice, finding it unbelievable that she had thought this kindly woman an enemy then. Her own mind, her own body were the greatest enemies certainly. Yet in the process of conquering, of understanding, she had grown to take a certain pride in her physical assets. She did not need a mirror to check the make-up on her face. A lighter shade of lipstick emphasized the color of her eyes instead of the heavy application of mascara. And the dresses she wore did not cling so tightly. Only by implication did they reveal that she was well built and desirable. She was a different person from the desperate, suicidal creature who had flung herself on Dr. Ross's mercy. Fingering again an old copy of *Time,* she knew she could read it now and concentrate without the grip of fear crushing her mentality.

And then the nurse cradled the receiver and made a note in her appointment book, just as she had probably done the first time Sue Ellen called. The office routine went on and on, ready to help another confused soul battling to gather courage and accomplish that first visit. Her glance passed over the red leather chairs, their cushions a little worn, but still sturdy. Someone had placed rhododendrons on the windowsill, she noticed, feeling pleasure in the touch of greenery behind the small wooden desk. Yes, everything must change, she thought. But how much changes for the better? A little thrill of joy passed through her to know that she was one of the fortunate ones.

Sue Ellen buttoned her sport coat. " 'Bye now," she said to the nurse who had turned her chair to the typewriter.

"See you on Thursday, Miss Gaynor?"

A confident smile tilted the corners of Sue Ellen's mouth. "Of course," she said.

The End